JERRY SPINELLI
LOSER

JOANNA COTLER BOOKS

An Imprint of HarperCollins*Publishers*

In some ways the writing of this book was a family affair.
Son Jeff James brought the Waiting Man to my attention; daughter-in-law Janet and grandson Zachary James helped with school matters,
as did son Ben Spinelli. My favorite mailmen were a big help:
Larry Lindeman and Jim Small. Thanks also to Dee Lindeman,
Mary Myers and Denise E. Franklin. A lifelong inspiration,
Nevin Hopple, finds a place in the story. My editors, my other eyes,
were Joanna Cotler and my wife, Eileen.

Loser
Copyright © 2002 by Jerry Spinelli
For information address HarperCollins Children's Books, a division of HarperCollins
Publishers, 1350 Avenue of the Americas, New York, NY 10019.
www.harperchildrens.com
Library of Congress Cataloging-in-Publication Data
Spinelli, Jerry.
  Loser / by Jerry Spinelli.
    p.   cm.
  Summary: Even though his classmates from first grade on have considered him strange
and a loser, Donald Zinkoff's optimism and exuberance and the support of his loving
family do not allow him to feel that way about himself.
  ISBN 0-06-000193-3 — ISBN 0-06-000483-5 (lib. bdg.)
  [1. Self-acceptance—Fiction.   2. Family life—Fiction.   3. Schools—Fiction.]   I.
Title.
PZ7.S75663 Lo   2002   2001047484
[Fic]—dc21   CIP
                                                                              AC
Typography by Alicia Mikles
4 5 6 7 8 9 10 ❖ First Edition

Pop

1 · You Grow Up

You grow up with a kid but you never really notice him. He's just there—on the street, the playground, the neighborhood. He's part of the scenery, like the parked cars and the green plastic cans on trash day.

You pass through school—first grade, second grade—there he is, going along with you. You're not friends, you're not enemies. You just cross paths now and then. Maybe at the park playground one day you look up and there he is on the other end of the seesaw. Or it's winter and you sled to the bottom of Halftank Hill, and you're trudging back up and there he goes zipping down, his arms out like a swan diver, screaming his head off. And maybe it annoys you that he seems to be having even more fun than you, but it's a one-second thought and it's over.

You don't even know his name.

And then one day you do. You hear someone say a name, and somehow you just know that's who the name belongs to, it's that kid.

Zinkoff.

2 · The Bright Wide World

He is one of the new litter of boys tossed up by this brick-and-hoagie town ten miles by trolley from a city of one million. For the first several years they have been home babies—Zinkoff and the others— fenced in by walls and backyard chain-link and, mostly, by the sound of Mother's voice.

Then comes the day when they stand alone on their front steps, blinking and warming in the sun like pups of a new creation.

At first Zinkoff shades his eyes. Then he lowers his hand. He squints into the sun, tries to outstare the sun, turns away thrilled and laughing. He reaches back to touch the door. It is something he will never do again. In his ears echo the thousand warnings of his mother: "Don't cross the street."

There are no other constraints. Not a fence in sight. No grown-up hand to hold. Nothing but the bright wide world in front of him.

He lands on the sidewalk with both feet and takes off. Heedless of all but the wind in his ears, he runs. He cannot believe how fast he is running. He cannot believe how free he is. Giddy with freedom and speed, he runs to the end of the block, turns right and runs on.

His legs—his legs are going so fast! He thinks that if they go any faster he might begin to fly. A white car is coming from behind. He races the car. He is surprised that it passes him. Surprised but not unhappy. He is too free to be unhappy. He waves at the white car. He stops and looks for someone to laugh with and celebrate with. He sees no one, so he laughs and celebrates with himself. He stomps up and down on the sidewalk as if it's a puddle.

He looks for his house. It is out of sight. He screams into the never-blinking sun: "Yahoo!" He runs some more, turns right again, stops again. It occurs to him that if he keeps turning right he can run forever.

"Yahoo!"

3 · Win

Sooner or later the let-loose sidewalk pups will cross the streets. Running, they will run into each other. And sooner or later, as surely as noses drip downward, it will no longer be enough to merely run. They must run against something. Against each other. It is their instinct.

"Let's race!" one will shout, and they race. From trash can to corner. From stop sign to mail truck.

Their mothers holler at them for running in the streets, so they go to the alleys. They take over the alleys, make the alleys their own streets.

They race. They race in July and they race in January. They race in the rain and they race in the snow. Although they race side by side, they are actually racing away from each other, sifting themselves apart. I am fast. You are slow. I win. You lose. They forget, never to remember again, that they are pups from the same litter.

And they discover something: They like winning more than losing. They *love* winning. They love winning so much that they find new ways to do it:

Who can hit the telephone pole with a stone?

Who can eat the most cupcakes?

Who can go to bed the latest?

Who can weigh the most?

Who can burp the loudest?

Who can grow the tallest?

Who is first . . . first . . . first . . . ?

Who?

Who?

Who?

Burping, growing, throwing, running— everything is a race. There are winners every- where.

I win!

I win!

I win!

The sidewalks. The backyards. The alleyways. The playgrounds. Winners. Winners.

Except for Zinkoff.

Zinkoff never wins.

But Zinkoff doesn't notice. Neither do the other pups.

Not yet.

4 · Zinkoff's First Day

Zinkoff gets in trouble his first day of school.

In fact, before he even gets to school he's in trouble. With his mother.

Like the other neighborhood mothers of first-day, first-grade children, Mrs. Zinkoff intends to walk her son to school. First day is a big day, and mothers know how scary it can be to a six-year-old.

Zinkoff stands at the front window, looking at all the kids walking to school. It reminds him of a parade.

His mother is upstairs getting dressed. She calls down, "Donald, you *wait*!" Her voice is firm, for she knows how much her son hates to wait.

By the time she comes downstairs, he's gone.

She yanks open the door. People are streaming by. Mothers hold the hands of younger kids while fourth- and fifth-graders yell and run and rule the sidewalks.

Mrs. Zinkoff looks up the street. In the distance she sees the long neck of a giraffe poking above the crowd, hurrying along with the others. It's him. Must be him. He loves his giraffe hat. His dad bought it for him at the zoo. If she has told him once, she has told him fifty times: Do *not* wear it to school.

The school is only three blocks away. He will be there before she can catch him. With a sigh of surrender she goes back into the house.

The first-grade teacher stands at the doorway as her new pupils arrive. "Good morning . . . Good morning . . . Welcome to school." When she sees the face of a giraffe go by, she nearly swallows her greeting. She watches the giraffe and the boy under it march straight to a front-row desk and take a seat.

When the bell rings, the teacher, Miss Meeks, shuts the door and stands before the desk of the unusually hatted student. The other students are openly giggling. She wonders if this boy is going to be a problem. This is Miss Meeks's year to retire, and the last thing she needs is a troublesome first-grader.

"That's quite a hat you have there," she says. It is in fact remarkably lifelike.

The boy pops to his feet. He beams. "It's a giraffe."

"So I see. But I'm afraid you'll have to take it off now. We don't wear hats in the classroom."

"Okay," he says cheerfully. He takes off the hat.

"You may be seated."

"Okay."

He seems agreeable enough. Perhaps he will not be troublesome after all.

Now she has to tell him that he cannot keep the hat with him. She hopes he won't break out bawling. First-graders can be so unpredictable. You never know what might set them off.

She tells him. She keeps an eye on his lower lip, to see if it will quiver. It does not. Instead he pops to his feet again and brightly chirps, "Yes, ma'am," and hands the hat to her.

Yes, ma'am? Where did that come from? She smiles and whispers, "Thank you. Down now."

He whispers back, "Yes, ma'am."

Twenty-six heads turn to follow her as she carries the three-foot hat to the cubbyholes at the back of the room. She labeled the cubbies the day before, and now she suddenly realizes she doesn't know which one belongs to the boy. She turns. "What's your name, young man?"

He jumps to attention and belts at full voice, "Zinkoff!"

She has to turn her face to keep from laughing out loud. In all her thirty years of teaching, she has never known a student to announce himself or herself in such a manner.

She turns back to him and gives a slight bow, which somehow seems to be called for. "Thank you. And no need to shout, Mr. Zinkoff. Do you have a first name?"

The class is atwitter.

"Donald," he says.

"Thank you, Donald. And you may keep your seat. There is no need to rise when you speak."

"Yes, ma'am."

The cubbies, as the classroom seating soon will be, are in alphabetical order. She goes straight to the last cubbyhole and inserts the giraffe. The space is not deep enough to hold it all. It looks as if a baby giraffe is napping in there. The thought comes to her that Donald Zinkoff, in more ways than cubbyholes, will always be easy to find.

5 · All Aboard

Miss Meeks stands at the head of the class and for the thirty-first and last time gives her famous opening day speech:

"Good morning, young citizens . . ."

It pleases her to think that many years down the road a student or two might recall that Miss Meeks called them "young citizens" in the first grade. She feels that America's children are babied a bit too much and way too long.

"Welcome to your first day at John W. Satterfield Elementary School. This is a big, big day for you. Not only is it the first day of the school year, it is the first day of *twelve* school years. Hopefully, twelve years from now, every one of you will graduate from high school. That sounds like forever from now, doesn't it?"

A sea of nodding heads, as always.

"But it will come. Twelve years from now will surely come, and you will have learned how to write a topic sentence. And how to solve an equation. And even how to spell the word . . ." she pauses dramatically, she opens her eyes wide as if seeing the wonderful future . . . "tintinnabulation."

Audible gasps come from the sea of wide-eyed, oh-mouthed faces. A few shake their heads in vigorous denial. She sneaks a peek at Donald Zinkoff. He alone is grinning, giggling actually, as if he has been tickled.

"By the time you graduate from high school, many of you will already be driving cars and holding jobs. You will be ready to take your places in the world. You will be ready to travel all the way across the country by yourself, if you wish. Or to another country. You will be ready to begin your own families.

"What a wonderful adventure it will be! And it all begins here. Right now. Today. It will be a journey and an adventure of many days." She pauses. She holds out her arms. "'How many days?' you ask."

Several hands shoot up. She knows if she answers them, someone will knock her whole point out of whack with a guess in the millions. She ignores them. She goes to the board. With a new-year, crisply cut length of chalk, she writes in large numbers on the green slate:

$$180$$

"That," she says, "is the number of days we are required to be in school each year."

She turns back to the greenboard. Under the 180 she writes:

$$\times 12$$

"That is the number of years you will attend school. Now let's multiply."

She does the math on the greenboard, writing the numbers slowly, grandly:

$$
\begin{array}{r}
180 \\
\times 12 \\
\hline
360 \\
180 \\
\hline
2160
\end{array}
$$

She points to the bottom number. "There it is." She taps the greenboard twice with the chalk. "Two thousand one hundred and sixty. The days of your journey. That is how long your adventure will last. Every one of those days will be an opportunity to learn something new. Just *imagine* how much you can learn in two thousand one hundred and sixty days!"

She pauses to let them imagine.

"Two thousand one hundred and sixty adventures. Two thousand one hundred and sixty opportunities to become whatever you want to become. This is what you've been waiting six years for. This is the day it begins."

She wishes she had a camera.

She looks at the clock above the door. She acts surprised. "Oh my goodness! Look at that! Time is passing! Before you know it, there will only be two thousand one hundred and fifty-nine days left. Our first day is passing by and we haven't even learned a thing yet! What do you say we get this learning train started?"

She reaches into her desk drawer and pulls out the old, navy blue train conductor's cap. For the thirty-first and last time she puts it on. She pumps her hand twice. "Toot! Toot! All aboard the Learning Train! First stop, Writing My Own Name! Who's coming aboard?"

Twenty-six hands shoot into the air. And Zinkoff, jumping to his feet so fast that he knocks his desk over with a nerve-slapping racket, thrusts up his hands and bellows to the ceiling: *"YAHOO!"*

6 · A Wonderful Question

Donald Zinkoff

Before arriving in first grade, he has learned his letters. Some of them, anyway. And of course he has seen his name from time to time. But he has never traced it on see-through paper. He has never tried to copy it, has never hitched a ride on a pencil point, feeling the shape and movement of his name's letters.

Don

Now, as he moves the pencil across the blue lines of the paper, he feels a thrill. He stares at his name, and it is as if he is staring at himself. As if the Donald Zinkoff that was born six years ago is here and now, by his own hand, in some small way being born all over again.

He rushes up to the teacher. He shoves the paper in her face. "Look! It's me!"

She takes the paper. At the top is his name as she has spelled it out for him to copy, as she has done for all of the students. Below that is his own attempt. If she didn't know what it was supposed to say, she could never read it. The confusion of pencil lines on the paper makes no more sense than the playpen doodlings of a two-year-old.

The joy streaming up from his face makes her smile. She lays a hand on his shoulder. "To be perfectly precise about it," she says, "it is not you, it is your name. Your name is very important. It represents you."

"What does 'represents' mean?" he says.

"That means it takes your place. It sort of substitutes for you. Even when you yourself are not in a particular place, your name can be there. And so it's important to write it properly." She hands the paper back to him. "And to write it properly, you must practice. Use both sides."

A hundred sides would not have made a difference. Collecting papers before recess, she discovers that she still cannot read Donald Zinkoff's name. Of itself, this is no big deal. He certainly isn't the first sloppy handwriter she has come across. In the past she has had straight A students who could not seem to write a legible word. On the other hand, sometimes poor penmanship indicates a problem with motor skills. For the boy's sake, she hopes he is simply sloppy.

Recess!

At exactly 10 A.M. Zinkoff bursts onto the playground with the other Satterfield first-, second- and third-graders. For the first minute he is disappointed. He expected recess to be something different, something new. It turns out to be simply free time. Recess turns out to be just another name for life as he has always known it. Only shorter. His first recess lasted six years. This one is fifteen minutes. He means to make the most of it.

He dashes back into school. No one stops him. No one sees him. No one has ever run back *into* school during recess. He pulls his giraffe hat from the cubbie and runs back out to the playground.

"Hey, there he is!" someone shouts. "The kid with the hat!"

In seconds there's a crowd around him, kids reaching up to touch the hat, kids calling, "Can I wear it?"

And then the hat is gone, snatched from his head. A boy has it, he's running off with it, jamming it onto his own head. Now other hands are reaching, grabbing, snatching. The hat goes from head to head. The kids are screaming, laughing. A second-grader runs off with it. He goes galloping around the playground. The brown and yellow hat bobs on his head like a real giraffe. Zinkoff laughs aloud. He enjoys the spectacle so much that he forgets the hat is his.

And then a tall red-haired boy, a fourth-grader, stands in front of the galloper, holding out his hand. The second-grader takes off the hat and hands it over. The red-haired fourth-grader looks at the hat carefully. Instead of putting it on his head, he sticks his arm into it, all the way up to his shoulder. With his fingers inside the head, he makes the giraffe nod and seem to talk. He walks over to one of his equally tall friends. He makes the giraffe's mouth clamp onto his friend's nose. Everybody laughs. Zinkoff laughs. Even the recess-duty teacher laughs.

The boy turns to the first-graders, who are keeping their distance. "Whose hat is this?"

Zinkoff runs forward. He trips over a foot and falls flat on his face. Everybody laughs. Zinkoff laughs. He comes up to the tall red-haired boy. He stands much closer than a first-grader normally gets to a fourth-grader. He looks directly up into the tall boy's face and proudly announces, "It's my hat."

The boy smiles. He shakes his head slowly. "It's *my* hat."

Zinkoff just stares up. He is fascinated by the boy's face. He has never seen a face smile and shake itself no at the same time.

And he realizes that apparently there has been a mistake. Perhaps the tall boy was at the zoo on the same day Zinkoff was there. Perhaps he bought the giraffe hat first and left it behind by mistake. Whatever, there is no mistaking what the boy said: "It's *my* hat."

Zinkoff is sad. He has really come to love the hat that he thought was his. But he is not sad too, because he can tell how happy it makes the tall boy to get his hat back.

The boy is still smiling down at him. Zinkoff already knows that smiles do not like to be alone, so he sends his best smile up to join the one above. "Okay," he says cheerfully.

The smile on the tall boy's face twists and changes. Zinkoff does not know it, but he has just cheated the boy. The boy expected Zinkoff to make a fuss, to try to get his hat back, maybe even to cry or pitch a fit. The boy loves to see first-graders pitch fits. It's fun. And now he is cheated of his fun, cheated by this smiling, agreeable little insect in front of him.

The tall boy takes off the hat. He pokes Zinkoff in the forehead with one of the giraffe's horns. "It's not mine, you dummy." He wags his head and snickers. He turns to his friends. "First-graders are so dumb." His friends laugh. He throws the hat to the ground. As he walks off, he makes sure to step on it.

Zinkoff picks up the hat. Pieces of grit cling to the fuzzy surface. Suddenly the tall boy turns and looks back. Zinkoff drops the hat in case the boy wishes to step on it again. But the boy only laughs and goes away.

Zinkoff's mother is waiting for him after school. All the way home he jabbers about his incredible first day.

"Do you like your teacher?" she asks him.

"I love my teacher!" he says. "She called us 'young citizens'!"

She pats the top of his hat, which makes him almost as tall as her. "One thousand congratulations to you."

He beams. "Do I get a star?"

"I believe you do." His mother always carries with her a plastic Baggie of silver stars. She takes one out, licks it and presses it onto his shirt. "There."

As he bows his head to look at the star, the hat

topples from his head. His mother picks it up. She puts it on her own head. Zinkoff howls and claps. She wears it the rest of the way home.

Later Zinkoff sits on the front step waiting for his father to come home from work. His father is a mailman. He walks all day on his job but drives to and from the post office in his clunker. The Zinkoffs cannot afford a new car, so Mr. Zinkoff buys used ones. Every time he buys one he gets excited. "She's a real honeybug," he says. And then, a month or two later, every time, the honeybug starts to go bad. A retread tire loses its rubber. The carburetor starts coughing. The belts break. He keeps patching it up with duct tape, baling wire and chewing gum. Pretty soon everything is patches except Mr. Z's faith in his honeybug.

The day always comes when Mrs. Z whispers to her son, "It's another clunker." Zinkoff giggles and nods, but he never says the word "clunker" to his father, as that might hurt his feelings. It is never long after Mrs. Z says "clunker" that the car dies, usually on a rainy morning on the way to work. The car simply refuses to move another inch over the face of this earth, and even Mr. Z knows that it is beyond the help of even a thousand new plugs of chewing gum. The next day he gets rid of it and begins shopping for a new honeybug.

This cycle has happened four times so far, which is why Zinkoff mother and son, between the two of them, call the current car "Clunker Four."

Zinkoff hears Clunker Four long before he sees it. It makes a high squeal that reminds him of elephants in the movies. He runs to the curb as the car rounds the corner and rattles to a stop. As usual there is a smell of something burning in the air. "Daddy," he cries out, jumping into his father's arms, "I went to school!"

"And a star to prove it," says his father, hoisting him into the house.

Zinkoff talks about his first day at the dinner table and after dinner and right up until bedtime. As always, the last thing his mother says to him at night is, "Say your prayers." While she hides his giraffe hat in the trunk with the comforters and fancy tablecloth, Zinkoff transfers the star from his school shirt to his pajamas. He climbs into bed and tells God all about his first day. Then he tells the stars.

At this time in his life Zinkoff sees no difference between the stars in the sky and the stars in his mother's plastic Baggie. He believes that stars fall from the sky sometimes, and that his mother goes around collecting them like acorns. He believes she has to use heavy gloves and dark sunglasses because the fallen stars are so hot and shiny. She puts them in the freezer for forty-five minutes, and when they come out they are flat and silver and sticky on the back and ready for his shirts.

This makes him feel close to the unfallen stars left in the sky. He thinks of them as his night-lights. As he grows drowsy in bed, he wonders which is greater: the number of stars in the sky or the number of school days left in his life? It's a wonderful question.

7 · Jabip

Here is the surprise: Every day is like the first day to Zinkoff. Things keep happening that rekindle the excitement of the first day. Learning to read his first two-syllable word. Making a shoe-box scene about the Pilgrims. Counting to five in Spanish. Learning about water and ants and tooth decay. His first fire drill. Making new friends.

At the dinner table Zinkoff tells his parents about his days. But he always waits for his father's question. "So, what's new, Chickamoo?" Or "What's new, Boogaloo?" Or "Kinkachoo." Or "Pookypoo." Many things tickle Zinkoff, but nothing more than the sound of a funny word. Words tickle him like fingertips in the ribs. Every time his father comes up with a new one, Zinkoff has to put down his fork and laugh. Usually he leans to one side, as if the funny word has the force of a great wind. Sometimes he even falls off his chair.

It's his teacher, Miss Meeks, who comes up with the best one. She stands at the greenboard one day, trying to explain what a billion basketballs would look like. "If you put the first one here," she says, pointing to the floor, "and line them up out the door and down the hallway and across the playground and down the street—why, they would stretch from here to Jabip!"

The classroom is a sea of boggling eyes. Wow!

Someone calls out, "Where's Jabip?"

Miss Meeks explains that there is no actual place called Jabip. It's just her way of saying someplace really far away.

At that point Zinkoff, in the last seat in the last row, tilts alarmingly to the left and falls from his chair. The teacher rushes to him. His face is red. Tears stream down his cheeks. He's gasping for breath.

"Donald! Donald!" she calls, though he is inches away.

He looks up at her through watery eyes. He gasps, "Jabip!" He pounds the floor.

That's when Miss Meeks realizes her pupil isn't dying, he's merely laughing.

It's a good five minutes before Zinkoff calms down enough for the class to continue. Miss Meeks forbids the class—and herself—to utter the word "Jabip" for the rest of the day. Nevertheless, from time to time there are sudden giggly eruptions from the back row as the word pops back into Zinkoff's head.

When he hears Clunker Four coming that day, he runs alongside the car as it coasts to the curb. "Daddy! Daddy! Did you ever hear of Jabip?"

"Sure," says his father out the open window. "I also heard of Jaboop."

Zinkoff rolls on the sidewalk. Jabip. Jaboop. He keeps erupting through dinner. Eating becomes hazardous. His parents smile patiently for the first minute or so, then begin telling him enough is enough. But Zinkoff can't stop. When a bolt of mashed potatoes shoots from his nose, he is sent to his room. That night he giggles through his prayer and into sleep.

In school for the rest of the week Zinkoff continues to produce outbursts of laughter in the back row. Every outburst triggers laughter from the other pupils. Sometimes, to get him started, a pupil waits until the teacher's head is turned, then whispers the forbidden word. Sometimes Miss Meeks bites her tongue to keep from joining in, sometimes she gets mad.

It's during one of the mad times that she says, "Donald, come up here, please." When he stands before her she takes something from her desk drawer. It's a round yellow button. It's the largest button the students have ever seen, as large as a giant pinwheel taffy. It has black letters on it. "Can you tell me what it says?"

Zinkoff studies the button. Finally he shakes his head.

"It says, 'I know I can behave.'" She pins the button onto his shirt. "And I know you can."

Zinkoff has to wear the button for an hour. During that time he does not laugh once. Miss

Meeks judges her maneuver a success and returns the button to the drawer. Soon Zinkoff is laughing again. He gets the button back.

So it goes for several days. Second-graders who wore the button the previous year and who have heard of Zinkoff's endless giggling ask him in the playground, "Did you get the button today?"

One day Miss Meeks has to leave the classroom for a while. When she returns she finds Zinkoff's hand waving in the air.

"Yes, Donald?"

"Miss Meeks," he says, "I laughed when you were gone."

And she realizes at last that for Zinkoff the button is not a punishment at all, but a badge of honor. From then on she punishes him by keeping the button in the drawer.

Button or no button, Zinkoff loves school. One day he awakes before anyone else in the house. He gets himself dressed. He makes his own breakfast. He brushes his teeth and walks off to school. *I must be early*, he thinks, for he sees no crossing guards or other children along the way.

He is sitting on the front step waiting for the door to open when he hears Clunker Four. It stops in front of the school and out pop both his mother and father. Both come running.

"Donald, we've been looking all over! You weren't in your bed!"

"I came to school all by myself," he declares proudly.

His parents look at each other. His mother bites her lip. His father picks him up and says, "You're very big to do that all by yourself. The only problem is, there's no school today. It's Saturday."

When Miss Meeks passes Zinkoff on to second grade, she writes on the back of his final report card: "Donald sometimes has a problem with self-control, and I wish he were neater, but he is so good-natured. That son of yours is one happy child! And he certainly does love school!"

8 · Two New Friends

In the summer between first and second grades Zinkoff acquires two new friends. One is a baby sister, the other is a neighbor. The baby sister is Polly. The neighbor is Andrew.

When Zinkoff first meets the baby, his mother says, "Look," and pulls down the blanket. Zinkoff's eyes boggle. There are two silver stars on the baby's diaper. This baby is less than one day old. What can she have done already to deserve two stars? He's never been awarded more than one at a time. "Mom," he says, "*two* stars? What did she *do*?"

"She did the best thing of all," says his mother, pulling up the blanket. "She was born."

Has Zinkoff been misinformed? "I was born too, wasn't I?"

She pats his hand. "Absolutely. You were every bit as born as Polly was."

"So," he says, "how come I didn't get two stars?"

"Who says you didn't?"

He brightens. "I did?"

She shakes her head. "Sorry. I was kidding you. That was before I started giving out stars." Now she needs to pick him up again. "Tell you what—how would you like your being-born stars now? Better late than never."

He brightens again. "Yeah!"

But she's not finished thinking. "Or how about this? We could make a deal. We could wait until you're having a really bad day, some day when you could really, really use two stars to pick you up. That's when you get them."

He thinks it over. He hates to wait, but he loves to make deals. "Okay," he says and shakes his mother's hand. Then he reaches into the blanket and shakes the baby's foot.

A month later the new neighbors move in next door. That same day Mrs. Zinkoff bakes a strawberry angel food cake and carries it out the front door. Her firstborn tags along. "This is how we say welcome," she says.

He stands at his mother's side as she rings the doorbell and says, "Welcome to the neighborhood" and hands the cake to the new lady neighbor, whose proper name is Mrs. Orwell, but whose first name is better: Cherise. Then he is introduced. "This is my son, Donald."

Cherise smiles down at him and shakes his hand and says, "Hello, Donald. I have a son too. His name is Andrew. How old are you?"

"Six," he replies.

"So is Andrew."

Zinkoff stares at the two ladies in wonder. "Wow! Same as me!" He looks past Cherise. "Is he in there?"

"He is," says Cherise, "but he's hiding. He says he's never coming out. He's mad because we moved away from our other house."

Zinkoff thinks about this for a moment. He lifts a finger to Cherise. "I have an idea. Tell Andrew my father is a mailman. That will make him come out." In Zinkoff's view, carrying the mail is the most interesting job there is.

Cherise nods solemnly. "I'll give it a try."

Before Zinkoff and his mother get back to their own house, he has another idea. "I'm going to make a special welcome just for Andrew."

"Good for you," says his mother. "A cake?"

"No, a cookie."

His mother does not say no. His parents try not to say no to him unless it's really necessary. So when he announces that he intends to bake a cookie, his mother simply says, "What kind?"

He doesn't hesitate. "A snickerdoodle!" The snickerdoodle is his favorite cookie. Every cookie tastes good to him, but snickerdoodles taste twice as good because of their name. Sometimes his dad says "snookerdiddle" and makes him laugh for an hour.

Zinkoff's idea is to bake a snickerdoodle so big that Andrew the new neighbor will *have* to come out and see it.

Since he is working on the kitchen table, it seems to him that the largest cookie he can make would be one as large as the table itself. But his mother points out that a cookie that big could not fit in the oven. So he settles for a rectangular cookie that covers the entire cookie pan.

Every time his mother tries to help, the young chef snaps at her, "I can do that." So his mother simply gives directions and says "Heaven help me" a lot while her intrepid son makes a mess of the kitchen. Flour and eggs fly everywhere. For weeks to come the family will feel the crunch of sugar grains underfoot.

Finally, miraculously, the cookie gets baked. He snatches the quilted mitten and potholder from his mother—"I can *do* it *myself*"—pulls the hot pan from the oven and sets it on the kitchen table. Impatient as always, he cannot wait for it to cool. He blows over the steaming cookie until he's out of breath. He flaps his hands over it. At last the pan is cool enough to touch without the mitten.

He runs next door with it. He rings the bell. Cherise opens the door.

"Hi, Donald."

"Hi, Cherise. I made a welcome cookie for Andrew. It's a snickerdoodle. I think if you put it on the floor and wait a little while, he'll smell it and come out."

Zinkoff is utterly serious, but for some reason Cherise laughs. "Come on in," she says. "Wait here."

Cherise leaves him standing in the living room. He hears whispery voices upstairs. Once he hears a sharp "No!" Then there are footsteps on the stairs, and here at last is Andrew Orwell walking toward him in his grumpy face and pajamas in the middle of the day.

"Hi," Zinkoff says. "My name is Donald Zinkoff. I'm your neighbor. I made you a welcome cookie. It's a snickerdoodle."

Andrew's face perks up. He leans in to smell the cookie. He is hooked.

Zinkoff reaches for the spatula his mother told him to bring along. A cookie is not really a cookie until it's out of the pan and into the hand. He lays the pan on the floor. He pries the giant snickerdoodle from the sides and bottom of the pan. He lifts out the warm, soft, heavenly smelling welcome. He lifts it with both hands and holds it out to Andrew. As Andrew reaches for it, the panless, unsupported cookie collapses of its own weight and falls to the floor. Zinkoff is left with a bite-size scrap in each hand.

Andrew Orwell stares in horror at the floor. He screams, "My cookie!" He screams at Zinkoff. "You dropped it!" He runs screaming up the stairs. "I hate this place!"

Zinkoff stuffs one scrap into his mouth, then the other. He gathers up the collapsed pieces from the floor and carries them home in the pan. He sits on the front step. Everybody who passes by that afternoon is offered a piece of cookie. In between, Zinkoff helps himself.

By the time Clunker Four rattles up to the curb, the cookie is gone. As his father gets out of the car, Zinkoff runs to him, plunges his head into his father's mailbag and throws up.

Zinkoff was born with an upside-down valve in his stomach. This causes him to throw up several times a week. To Zinkoff, throwing up is almost as normal as breathing.

But not to his father, who has brought his mailbag home with him in order to repair the strap. When Donald was an infant, Mr. Zinkoff was very good about changing diapers, but he has no stomach for vomit. He turns away, holds out the bag and growls, "Take it to your mother."

Early on, Zinkoff's mother impressed upon her son the etiquette of throwing up: That is, do not throw up at random, but throw up *into* something, preferably a toilet or bucket. Since toilets or buckets are not always handy, Zinkoff has learned to reach for the nearest container. Thus, at one time or other he has thrown up into soup bowls, flowerpots, wastebaskets, trash bins, shopping bags, winter boots, kitchen sinks and, once, a clown's hat. But never his father's mailbag.

He thinks his mother will say "Heaven help me" but she does not. She's cool. She puts down baby Polly and unloads the bag into the toilet. She scours it with a stiff bristle brush and hand soap. She rubs it with Marley's Leather Cream. She sweetens it with a splash of Mennen's aftershave and sets it into the playpen for baby Polly to crawl into.

Hungry again, Zinkoff eats a full dinner that night. And throws up into one of his socks.

"Heaven help me."

9 · Champions!

Soccer is Zinkoff's kind of game.

Baseball has too much waiting and too many straight lines. Shooting a basketball demands precision. Football is fun only for the ball carrier.

But soccer is free-for-all, as haphazard and slapdash as Zinkoff himself. He plays in the Peewee League in the autumn of his seventh year. His team is the Titans. Every Saturday morning he's the first one there, kicking pinecones around the field until the coaches show up.

Once the game begins, Zinkoff never stops running. He zigs and zags after the checkered ball like a fox after a field mouse—except he hardly ever catches up to it. Someone else always seems to reach it first. Zinkoff is forever swinging his foot at the ball a half second after it goes past him. He winds up kicking the shins, ankles and rear ends of the other players. Twice he's kicked the referee. Once, somehow, he kicked himself. His teammates rub their bruises and call him "Wild Foot."

To Zinkoff a net is a net. He doesn't much care which team the net belongs to. Several times during the season he kicks the ball at the wrong goal. Fortunately, he always misses.

The first game is against the Ramblers. When it's over, Zinkoff jumps up and down and pumps his fists as he has seen athletes do and yells "Yahoo!" He does not notice that he is the only Titan cheering. "What are you so happy for?" says Robert, one of his teammates. "We lost."

This is news to Zinkoff. Throughout the game, and even at the end, he has not thought about the score. Apparently, losing has made Robert very unhappy. It shows on his face. It shows in the way he's kicking at the turf. Zinkoff looks around. Other Titans are kicking turf or stomping their feet or pounding their thighs with their fists. Every Titan wears a sour puss.

And then the coach calls the Titans into a huddle and says, "Okay, on three, yea Ramblers. One, two, three—" Zinkoff bellows, "Yea Ramblers!" And adds, "You da man!"

"Yea Ramblers" barely crawls from the lips of the other Titans.

And then the coach is lining them up, and the Ramblers are in a line too, and the Titans and Ramblers are patting hands down the line like dominos, pat pat pat pat, no sour pusses on the Ramblers, who keep saying "Good game, good game, good game . . ." and Zinkoff is the only Titan saying "Good game" back.

And then the Titans are heading for their parents on the sidelines, and in order to show their parents what serious soccer players they are, they kick the turf some more and tear off their knee pads and shirts and throw them to the ground and stomp on them. One Titan even falls to his knees and bawls while pounding his head into the grass.

Zinkoff wants to be a good Titan. He kicks at some turf too. His mother and father look on with mouths agape as he tears off his shirt and shoes and finally his socks and stomps them all into the ground. He gets down on his knees and rips up grass and flings it into the air. He snatches the pacifier from baby Polly's mouth and hurls it onto the field. He pounds his fists into the ground and cries out, "No! No! No!"

By now other parents and players are watching.

Zinkoff's mother says, "Just what do you think you're doing?"

Zinkoff looks up from his knees. "I'm being mad because we lost."

Baby Polly is bawling.

"Well, you can start being madder, because this little demonstration will cost you your allowance for a week. And you have five seconds to bring that pacifier back."

Zinkoff is determined to become a better loser. In the following weeks he practices his losing in the backyard. But he never again gets a chance to show his stuff on Saturday, for the Titans win all the rest of their games.

No great thanks to Wild Foot.

One time, amazingly, he finds himself alone with the ball and a clear field ahead of him.

Propelled by an excitement of whistles and screams behind him, Wild Foot boots the ball on and on, never realizing he has long since gone out of bounds. He crosses two other soccer fields and is finally stopped in the parking lot.

On another occasion he throws up on the ball, which in turn causes two other players to throw up.

It is after this incident that several Titans ask the coach if Zinkoff can be traded to another team. They are soon glad it didn't happen.

The last game of the season comes down to a play-off between the Titans and the Hornets. The Hornets also have lost only one game. The winner will be champion.

The game goes as usual for Wild Foot. He runs around a lot. He swings his foot a lot but seldom connects with the ball. Sometimes he makes himself dizzy running in circles as he tries to keep up with the action swirling around him.

Late in the second half the score is still 0–0. Zinkoff is standing in front of the Hornets' net, wondering where the ball is, when suddenly it hits him in the head. It bounces into the net for a goal, and Zinkoff is instantly mobbed by cheering teammates. The final score is Titans 1, Hornets 0.

The Titans are Peewee champions!

The Titans go wild. They jump like kangaroos. They fall onto their backs and churn their legs in the air. They ride their parents' shoulders and thrust up their fingers and crow, "We're number one!"

Zinkoff goes wild too. He tries to stand on his head. He shouts into baby Polly's face "We're number one!" and makes her blink. He climbs onto his father's shoulders and proclaims to all the wide world: "We're number one!"

And then he looks down and sees the face of Andrew Orwell, his neighbor. Andrew is a Hornet. Zinkoff has never seen a sadder face in his life. It reminds him of a monkey's face. He begins to notice the other Hornets, in their black-and-yellow shirts. They are slumped on the grass. They are slumped over their parents' knees. Not one of them rides a shoulder. Every one is monkey-faced and crying and slumpy.

Then they give out the trophies. Every Titan

gets one. Zinkoff has never won a trophy before. It's a golden soccer player on a black pedestal with a golden soccer ball at his foot. It glows as if it has been painted in sunlight. It is the most beautiful thing he has ever seen.

Zinkoff sees the other Titans kissing their trophies, so he kisses his too. As he does so, he sees the Hornets slumping away to the parking lot.

And suddenly he's running, he's yelling, "Andrew! Andrew!" Cherise and Andrew turn in the parking lot. Zinkoff runs huffing up to them. "Andrew, here." He holds out the trophy. The look in Andrew's eyes tells him he has done the right thing. "You take it."

Andrew reaches for it, but his mother catches his wrist. "Donald, that is really nice of you, but you're the one who won it. Andrew will win a trophy of his own someday."

Andrew's fingers are curled like claws. They can feel the golden trophy inches away. As his mother leads him off to the car, he cries out, "I *want* it!"

That afternoon Zinkoff sits on his back step. The trophy is beside him, brighter than ever.

Zinkoff is playing a game he invented called Bugs on a Stick. In the next backyard Andrew sits cross-legged by a bed of purple pansies. He cradles his chin in his hands. His face is still sad.

Zinkoff calls, "Wanna play my game?"

Andrew shakes his head.

"Wanna go in the alley?"

Andrew shakes his head.

Zinkoff asks Andrew many questions, but all Andrew does is shake his head and look monkey-faced.

After a while Zinkoff gets tired of his game. He looks at Andrew. He can think of nothing else to say. By now Zinkoff is sad too. Not just because Andrew is sad, but for another reason: The soccer season is over. That has been the best part of it. Playing the games. He wishes he could make himself feel less sad.

He picks up his trophy and goes inside. A minute later he opens the back door and places the trophy on the step and goes back in.

When he comes out later that day, the trophy is gone.

10 · Atrocious

Second grade is no more than a minute old when Zinkoff gets off on the wrong foot with his teacher.

He asks her how many days of school are left. Not in this year but in all remaining eleven years. The teacher, whose name is Mrs. Biswell, thinks it is the most annoying, untimely question she has ever heard. Here she is, all bright and shiny for first day, and this kid in the front row can't wait till he graduates from high school. It's insulting and disrespectful. She comes closer than she ever has before to saying, "That's a dumb question." Instead, she says, "Don't worry about it. You'll be out of school soon enough."

Zinkoff has no intention of worrying about it. And he certainly doesn't want to be out of school. He simply wants to hear her say a really big number in the thousands, so he can feel that his days in school will never come to an end. He has thought every teacher starts out the school year like Miss Meeks, but now he guesses he was wrong.

In the meantime he is packed off to the far back corner, last seat—the boondocks—as Mrs. Biswell assigns seats by first letter, last name.

The next bad thing he does is laugh. This might have been okay, but, Zinkoff being Zinkoff, he doesn't stop laughing. And when he does stop, it isn't long before he begins again.

Part of this is his own fault. Zinkoff is an all-purpose laugher. Not only do funny things make him laugh, but nearly anything that makes him feel good might also make him laugh. In fact, sometimes bad things make him laugh. He laughs as naturally as he breathes.

One day in the playground, a third-grader, angered by the sound of Zinkoff laughing, grabs Zinkoff by the wrist and pulls his arm behind his back. The higher he pulls the wrist toward the shoulder blade, the louder Zinkoff laughs, even through his tears. In the end the third-grader becomes frightened and gives up.

Of course, Zinkoff's classmates know what an easy laugher he is, so whenever they wish to be entertained, all they have to do is get Zinkoff's attention and stick out a tongue or pretend to pick and flick a booger. For half the class the entertainment is not in hearing Zinkoff laugh but in seeing him get in trouble.

Mrs. Biswell does not like children. Although she never says this, everyone knows it. Everyone wonders why someone who does not like children ever became a teacher in the first place. As the years have gone by, Mrs. Biswell herself has begun to wonder. Once a year, at home, she wonders aloud why she ever became a teacher, but there is never an answer from her husband or her three cats.

It is widely believed that Mrs. Biswell never smiles. In fact, this is not true. Mrs. Biswell smiles perhaps five or six times a year, but her face is so stone-chiseled into a permanent scowl that her smile appears to be merely a tilting of the scowl.

It is therefore impossible to tell if Mrs.

Biswell is really mad by looking at her face. The key is her hands. Anger makes hooks of her fingers and clamps her hands together. As her anger rises, the gnarled hands begin to churn over each other as if she is washing them in gritty soap.

Nothing makes Mrs. Biswell madder than sloppiness. She has had many sloppy students before, but Zinkoff is in a class by himself. Especially with a pencil in his hand. His numbers are a disaster. His fives look like eights, eights look like zeros, fours look like sevens.

At least there are only ten numerals. The alphabet gives him twenty-six letters to butcher. And once she starts teaching cursive, she might as well try to teach a pickle to write. His o's are raisins, his l's are drunken chili peppers, his q's are g's and his g's are q's.

And lines! The boy never saw a blue line he couldn't miss. Over the line, under the line, perpendicular to the line—his letters swarm willy-nilly across the page like ants on a sidewalk.

The teacher asks for a volunteer to help Zinkoff. Andrew Orwell volunteers. For a half hour each day Andrew sits with Zinkoff and shows him how to make better letters and numbers. After a week, Zinkoff's writing is worse than ever. Andrew is fired.

After two months of the worst penmanship she has ever endured, the teacher wrings her hands and calls out to the boondocks: "Your handwriting is atrocious!"

Zinkoff beams, not knowing the meaning of the word. "Thank you!" he calls back.

"My handwriting is atrocious!" he announces to his parents at the dinner table that day. His father, seeing how proud his son is, replies, "One thousand congratulations."

His mother gives him a star.

In all ways that teacher Biswell can see, the Z boy is a shambles. She shudders to think what must happen when he is in the same room with a coloring book. He is even at odds with his own body—not rare among second-graders, certainly, but this boy takes the cake. Hardly a day goes by in which he does not fall flat on his face for no apparent reason.

When he isn't laughing he's flapping his hand in the air. He's forever asking questions, forever volunteering to answer. For every right answer, five are wrong. The more he gets wrong, the more he wants to answer. The better to be seen back in his last-of-the-alphabet desk, he sometimes crouches on his seat like a baseball catcher, stabbing his hand into the air and grunting aloud.

It is unthinkable to Mrs. Biswell that such a mediocre-to-poor student could actually like school, so she concludes that his antics and reckless enthusiasms are merely ploys to annoy her.

Even so, she might forgive him—forgive him the sloppiness and the clumsiness and the endless laughing and the general annoyance that he is, forgive him for being a child—had he possessed the one thing for which she has a weakness: brilliance.

Brilliance is the one thing that makes Mrs. Biswell happy. In fourth grade in her own childhood, in the second report period, she got all A's and won a prize in her school's science fair. Ever since, she has had the highest regard for academic achievement. In all her years of teaching, she could name only nine students who deserved to be called "brilliant."

Zinkoff is not one of them. Quizzes, tests, projects—he never earns an A, and only one or two B's. He might earn more C's if she could understand his answers. Typically, she throws up her hands and gives him a D.

And so, in all these ways Zinkoff grinds down the patience of Mrs. Biswell. He is the greenboard against which her stick of chalk is reduced day by day. By December it is a nub.

And then he ruins her eraser.

Mrs. Biswell has long loved her eraser. It is so much better than the cheap, flimsy things that come through school supplies. Its deep, firm pad of felt soaks up chalk dust like a sponge. It is the Rolls Royce of greenboard erasers. Ten years ago she put out her own money for it, and she expects it to last for ten more. Every Friday she takes it home and claps it against the back of the field-stone barbeque pit in her yard. No one but her is allowed to touch it. For that matter, no one but her is allowed to touch the greenboard or the chalk.

One day she comes back late from lunch to find Zinkoff writing at the greenboard. The students in their seats let out a collective gasp. Zinkoff merely smiles at her and keeps on writing.

"Stop!" she screeches.

He stops. He looks at her, his eyes round as quarters. Then, quicker than she can think, he grabs the eraser and begins swiping at the greenboard.

"Stop! Stop! Stop!" she screams.

The words hit Zinkoff like a bear paw. His body flinches in three directions, he drops the eraser to the floor and throws up all over it.

"Out! Out! Out!" screams Mrs. Biswell. She stands in the doorway pointing down the hall. "Get out of my classroom and never come back!"

Zinkoff gets out.

In a daze he leaves the room and walks down the hallway. He flinches one final time as the classroom door slams shut behind him. He walks until he comes to the door at the end of the hall. He opens it and goes outside and keeps on walking. He walks for a long time, feeling behind his head the pointing finger of Mrs. Biswell.

In time he finds himself home. His mother is looking at him with alarm. She is asking him where his winter coat is. She's telling him that he is trembling.

Mrs. Biswell tells the principal it was a mistake. She was merely pointing to the principal's office, she says, sending him there. The principal says mistake or not, no teacher can banish a student from school. Mrs. Biswell says she simply lost her temper, as anyone would have done if they had had to put up with *that* student. The principal says a teacher isn't just anyone, and he scolds her in the privacy of his office.

When Mrs. Zinkoff telephones the principal and asks if it's true that her son was told never to return to school, the principal laughs and says it was all a mistake and of course he is most welcome to come back. Zinkoff is back at school next day before the janitor.

For the rest of the school year Mrs. Biswell wrings her hands and combs the stores and catalogs for another Rolls Royce eraser. With her own money she buys Zinkoff a yellow plastic beach bucket. She tells him he is never to go anywhere inside her classroom without it. Zinkoff never throws up into the yellow bucket, but he does use it to carry around his collection of interesting stones and pieces of colored glass.

11 · Mailman

In the spring Mrs. Biswell is certain that Zinkoff will be absent at least one day: Take Your Kid to Work Day. The boy is forever blabbing about his father the mailman and that he himself is going to be a mailman when he grows up. Surely he will want to go to work with his father that day.

The teacher is both right and wrong. Zinkoff definitely wants to miss school on Take Your Kid to Work Day, but the post office will not allow children to accompany postal parents on their routes. They say it is too dangerous and, besides, the mail Jeeps have only one seat.

Zinkoff has been begging his father for years to take him to work. Now, the thought of watching other kids go off to work with their parents while he stays behind is too painful to bear. Every day he pesters his father.

"I can't," says his father. "They'll fire me. Do you want them to fire me?"

The youngster can only shake his head and pout. And the pestering starts all over.

Days of this.

At last Mr. Z has an idea.

"Okay, okay," he says. "I can't take you to work officially. I can't take you on a workday. I can't take you in the Jeep. So here's what we'll do . . ."

When Zinkoff hears his father's plan, he rushes next door to tell Andrew.

"I'm having my own day. Take Donald Zinkoff to Work Day. It's going to be on Sunday. Now I can do it and my dad won't get fired."

"I'm going with my dad on the real Take Your Kid to Work Day," says Andrew.

"My dad's a mailman," says Zinkoff. "I'm going to deliver mail."

"My dad's a banker," says Andrew. They are in Andrew's backyard. Andrew is batting a Ping-Pong ball against the wall with his mother's pancake spatula. He borrowed the Ping-Pong ball from Zinkoff weeks before. "I'm going to make money."

"I'm going to ride in my dad's clunker."

"I'm going to ride to work on the train. All the way to the city."

"I'm going to carry my dad's mailbag. He says it's really heavy, but I'm going to carry it."

Andrew turns and whacks the ball as hard and high as he can. It sails to the Zinkoffs' roof and rolls into the rain gutter. "I'm going to sit at my dad's desk. He said I can even sit in the vice president's chair."

Zinkoff stares up at the rain gutter. That was his only Ping-Pong ball. "I'm having lunch with my dad. We're going to eat right there in the Clunker."

"We're eating lunch in a restaurant. Sometimes the mayor goes there. My dad says when he gets a raise, we're outta here. He says we're never coming back to this dump."

Zinkoff looks around. He doesn't see any dump. He wonders what dump Andrew's father was talking about. He can't look up at the rain gutter without the sun blinding him.

When the official Take Your Kid to Work Day arrives, Zinkoff watches Andrew go off to the city with his dad. Andrew wears a suit and tie. He looks like a little banker.

Two days later, Sunday, is Take Donald Zinkoff to Work Day. To prepare for the day, Zinkoff's dad has brought him a tall stack of envelopes and sheets of paper. Since there is no official mail to deliver on a Sunday, Zinkoff has to make his own mail. He writes letters. Forty, fifty, sixty letters and more. He writes words that he imagines people say in letters. He feels really grown-up because the sheets of paper have no lines. He folds up the letters and puts them in the envelopes. He draws stamps in crayon in the upper right corners of the envelopes and writes addresses and puts the finished letters—one hundred of them!—into the mailbag.

The Zinkoff family goes to church early that Sunday. Two minutes after they get home, the town's newest mailman is ready. He takes the lunches from the refrigerator. They were packed the night before in two brown paper bags. He lets his dad carry the lunches. Himself he harnesses to the great leather bag. It hangs down to his heels. He hauls it across the living-room floor, out the door, down the front steps and across the sidewalk to the Clunker. Somehow he manages to sit in the car with the mailbag on his back.

Mr. Zinkoff is determined to make the day live up to his son's expectations. He knows Donald expects to travel a respectable distance to work, so he drives around for fifteen minutes before pulling into the empty parking lot of a dentist three blocks from their home. The street is called Willow.

Donald jumps from the car and starts off. His father grabs him. "Whoa there, Nellie."

He gives his son instructions. Start with the dentist. One letter to each house. No peeking in the mail slots. Act professional.

"What does 'act professional' mean?" Donald wants to know.

"It means behave like a grown-up doing a job. That's what you're getting paid for."

The boy gawks at his father. "I'm getting paid?"

"Sure. End of the day. Five bucks."

"Five bucks!" Donald tries to leap for joy, but the mailbag holds him down.

"And one more thing," says his father. "You can't be a real mailman without this." He reaches into the backseat and pulls out a hat. And not just any hat. His own mail carrier hat. The postal blue, strawlike pith helmet that he wears on hot summer days with his Bermuda shorts uniform.

Donald is popping with pride. He puts on the helmet. Of course, it's too big and comes down to his ears and nose, but he couldn't care less. He adjusts the helmet as best he can and staggers off to the dentist's door, the mailbag thumping against his heels. The helmet wobbles on his head.

He stops, turns. He calls, "And one *more* thing, Dad."

"What's that?"

"Be friendly. Mailmen are always friendly."

"That's right. Now get to work."

The dentist's mailbox is at the edge of the parking lot. Donald swings the bag around so he can reach inside, grabs a letter and places it in the box. He turns to his father in the car and raises his hands in triumph. "Yes!"

Ninety-nine to go.

He starts off down the block. A few of the houses on Willow are single homes with porches. The rest are brick row houses like his own. Some have mailboxes fixed to a railing. Some have slots in the front doors.

The first house has a slot. Donald slips a letter through. He listens for it to land but he cannot hear it. The slot is eye-high. Quietly, with his finger, he pushes in the swinging brass flap. He takes off his helmet and scrunches his eyeball to the slot and strains to see the letter on the floor. All he can make out is a green carpet. He looks around some more, hoping to spot something interesting, but all he sees is an ordinary living room with furniture and a picture on the wall of four basset hounds playing cards.

"No peeking!"

His father's voice pierces the jungle cat grumble of Clunker Four, prowling slowly along in the street. Donald lets the brass flapper swing down. He replaces his helmet and goes back to work.

He discovers one thing right away: It is usually more fun to deliver mail to a door slot than to a mailbox. With a mailbox, no one even knows you're delivering. But with a slot, you're dumping the letter smack into the people's house, and sometimes they're right there on the other side of the door and you can hear them.

"Mommy! Mommy! We got mail!" he hears on the other side of one door. He pauses on the front steps to listen.

"There's no mail on Sunday," comes a mother's cranky reply.

"Yes, there is! There's mail on Sunday! Look!"

Donald walks off smiling. He feels like Santa Claus.

At another house, just as he is about to push a letter through the slot, the door opens. Standing there is a two-year-old wearing nothing but a diaper and a mouth smeared with chocolate.

They stare at each other for a while, then

Donald says, "Mailman," and holds out the letter.

"Moommsh," says the two-year-old. Donald can't tell if it's a boy or girl. Whichever, its cheeks are bursting with food. The air is heavy with peanut butter.

"You take it," says Donald. "Maybe it's a letter for you."

The two-year-old takes it in chocolaty fingers. Suddenly he or she turns and runs, crying out, "Moommsh! Moommsh!"

Donald pulls the door shut.

Several houses later a kid is sitting on the top step. He looks like he's mad at somebody. The mailbox is bolted to the brick wall under the house numbers. Donald isn't sure what to do. Should he put the letter in the mailbox, or give it to the kid? But what if the kid doesn't live here?

"Do you live here?" says Donald.

The kid gives him a glare but no answer. The Clunker grumbles in the street.

Donald decides the kid probably does live here. He further decides that the professional thing to do will be to put the letter in the mailbox. He is reaching out to do so when the kid snatches the letter from his hand.

The kid looks at the envelope. He makes a face. "This ain't no letter."

"It's a letter," says Donald. "I'm delivering the mail. Look. This is my dad's mailbag."

"This ain't no *letter*," the kid repeats. His lip curls into a sneer when he says the word "letter." "This ain't no *stamp*. It's *crayon*. This ain't no ad*dress*. You can't even *read* it." He rips open the envelope. "And this ain't *writing*. It's *scribbles*." He rips the letter in half and stuffs it back into the leather bag.

Donald knows he's supposed to deliver the mail despite rain, sleet or snow—but what about mean big kids who tear your letter in pieces?

He turns his eyes to Clunker Four. His father gives him a thumbs-up and points to the next house.

Donald remembers: Be friendly.

He gives the kid his best smile. "Nice to meet you," he says and moves on.

Behind several doors he hears dogs barking.

Behind another he hears a language he doesn't recognize. He hears bits and pieces of words and people sounds, and, once, a noise that sounds exactly like that of a flying dinosaur he saw in the movies, but of course that couldn't be.

Each time he tries to sneak a peek through a mail slot, his father calls "No peeking!" But he can't help himself.

There is a minute or two during which he has a strange thought. Actually he doesn't really *have* the thought. His mind is trying to catch the thought as a cat tries to catch a shadow. The thought, if he could catch it, would go something like this: Behind the front doors of houses incredible, impossible things are happening, and as soon as you lift the mail flapper they all disappear and all you see is an ordinary living room.

When he comes to the last house in the second block—fifty-six homes so far and one dentist—his father calls out, "Lunchtime!"

12 · The Nine Hundred Block of Willow

His father parks the Clunker, and they sit in the front seat having lunch. Donald has given much thought to lunch. On an ordinary day he might have packed a peanut butter and banana sandwich and a pack of M&M's and a strawberry Twinkie. But that is not what a mailman would eat. So he made himself a sandwich of Lebanon baloney and cheese and lettuce and pickle chips and mustard. For dessert he chose an apple. He wanted to bring coffee in the thermos jug, but his mother would only allow decaffeinated iced tea.

It's the best lunch he's ever had, sitting in Clunker Four with his dad, pith helmet and leather bag waiting in the backseat. He pours iced tea into the red plastic cup and pretends it's coffee.

He eats half his sandwich, two bites of the apple and a sip of iced tea. As he opens the car door his father says, "Where are you going?"

"Back to work," says Donald. He can't wait. He's too excited to eat.

"Close the door. Relax," says his father. "You don't just wolf down your lunch and run off. Lunchtime is not for eating. Working man needs a break."

Donald closes the door. He sits back. He folds his arms. He looks at the ceiling. He whistles.

His father laughs. "Are you relaxing?"

"Yep."

"Well, we don't just relax. We talk too. We have a chat."

"What do we chat about?"

"Anything we want."

Donald doesn't have to think long. "Dad," he says, "do you think it's going to snow?"

"Someday, sure, next winter. But not today. We got a warm day in April here."

"Oh," says Donald. "How about rain?"

Mr. Zinkoff looks at the sky. "Doesn't look like it."

"Hail?" Donald says hopefully.

"Sorry."

Donald punches the seat cushion. "Phooey."

To Donald, one of the best things about being a mailman is that you have to deliver the mail in spite of snow, rain, hail and, for all he knows, tidal waves and tornadoes. In fact, it was on a day when he saw his father come home with icicles hanging from his earmuffs that he decided to become a mailman. He watched his father shake the snow and ice from himself, and he said, "Wow, Dad! Was it hard?" He has never forgotten the answer. His father picked an icicle from his hat, stuck it in his mouth like a toothpick and said, "Nah. No problem. Piece a cake." From that day on, when he sees stormy weather out the classroom window, he thinks of his dad trudging heroically through the blizzard saying, "Piece a cake . . . piece a cake . . ."

The night before, Donald went to bed fervently wishing for a blizzard the next day. When he awoke he ran to the window and was met by pure sunshine. He searched sky and ground for evidence of bad weather, but could not find so much as a solitary hailstone.

"But you know," says his father, "weather isn't the only thing you have to worry about."

"It's not?"

"No way. There's biting dogs and wild cats. There's banana peels you can slip on. There's turtles you can trip over and break your nose. There's rhinos."

Donald boggles. "Rhinos?"

"Sure. Who says a rhino can't escape from the zoo and show up on your mail route? Do you know of any law that says that can't happen?"

Donald couldn't think of a single law against it. "I guess not," he says.

His father nods. "There you go. It's a dangerous world out there. A mailman has more than just snow and rain to deal with."

Donald beams. "Yahoo!" He looks out the window, relieved to know the world is not as safe as it appears to be. "Is lunchtime over yet, Dad?"

Mr. Z consults his watch. "Almost. Just enough time to talk about the Waiting Man."

Donald stares. "Huh?"

"The Waiting Man. You'll see him in the next block, the nine hundred block. Nine twenty-four Willow. You can see him in the window behind the mailbox."

Donald is intrigued. "Is he waiting for the mail?"

"No, he's waiting for his brother. I hear he's been waiting for him for thirty-two years. His brother went away to fight in the Vietnam War and was MIA and never came back."

Donald senses a sadness somewhere in the distance. "What's 'MIA'?"

"Missing in action. It means they're pretty sure he was killed but they can't find his body."

"Are *you* pretty sure, Dad?"

His father looks out the window. He nods slowly. "I'm pretty sure."

"Isn't the Waiting Man pretty sure?"

"I guess not."

Thirty-two *years*. Donald cannot imagine it. Donald cannot wait more than thirty-two *seconds* for anything. Of course, a brother isn't just anything. Thirty-two years. Would he wait that long for a brother? Would he wait that long for Polly?

His father claps his hands. "Okay. Enough of this chitchat. Time to hit the trail. Let's go! People are waiting for their mail!"

Donald scrambles into the backseat. He

straps on the bag, plunks on his helmet and hits the sidewalk.

As it turns out, no escaped rhinos are out and about this particular day. No turtles either. Not even a banana peel. But Donald does see the Waiting Man. He's a face in the window next to the numbers white against the brick: 924. He appears to be wearing pajamas. His white hair is thick around his ears and wispy on top. He is looking up the street, in the direction that Donald came from. When Donald stands on the top step, he is close enough to reach out and touch the window. But the Waiting Man does not turn, does not seem to know Donald is there. He merely stares unblinking up the street.

Donald watches the Waiting Man for much longer than he realizes. He does not move away until, in his own mind, he has waited longer than he had ever waited for anything in his life.

He is at the next house before he realizes he has forgotten something. He rushes back to deliver 924 its letter. The Waiting Man is still there.

Several houses later Donald hears someone behind him calling: "Mailman! Oh mailman!"

He turns. He has to lift his head to see out from under the brim of the pith helmet.

A white-haired lady in a mint-green dress is standing on a step waving her letter. She is surrounded by a four-legged aluminum walker. She's smiling at him. "Thank you, mailman!" she calls.

Donald calls back, "You're welcome!" He stands at attention and salutes her.

Shortly after that comes a moment Donald has not expected. He reaches into the bag and feels nothing but leather. He takes it off and puts it on the sidewalk and peers into it. Nothing. Empty. He has delivered his one hundred letters. Many times he has imagined the start of Take Donald Zinkoff to Work Day; never has he imagined the end of it.

Clunker Four grumbles at the curb.

"Workday's over," calls his dad. "Time to go home."

Reluctantly Donald drags the bag to the car. He gets in. He does not take off the helmet. His father gives him his day's pay. He puts it in his pocket without looking at it. He cries all the way home.

13 · Waiting

Andrew's father must have gotten a raise, because by the time Zinkoff enters third grade, Andrew is gone. Moved. To a place outside of town called Heatherwood. To a house with a driveway and a front yard with a tree, Zinkoff hears.

In November of third grade Zinkoff goes through the worst period in all his eight years. He has surgery. He goes into the hospital and they put him to sleep and the doctor turns the upside-down valve in his stomach right-side up. The good news is that he stops throwing up. The bad news is that he has to miss three weeks of school.

He drives his mother crazy. "Heaven help me" every ten minutes. On the second day after returning home from the hospital, he tries to sneak off to school. So his mother creates an alarm. She places the alarm in front of the front door. If her son ever tries to leave, the alarm goes off. The alarm is Polly.

Polly is seventeen months old by now. She speaks very little at this point, but one thing she does say is "Bye-bye." She says it distinctly—in fact, she shouts it—and she says it whenever she sees someone leaving the house. Each morning Mother Zinkoff padlocks the back door. Then she wheels the playpen up against the front door and places Polly inside. Then she goes about her chores, ready to come running whenever she hears "Bye-bye!"

It happens only once. Mrs. Z comes running to find her son halfway out the door and Polly yelling "Bye-bye!" at the top of her lungs. She also finds a chocolate cupcake mashed in Polly's hand. A bribe.

Once Zinkoff understands that escape is impossible, he considers other ways to spend his time. This is critical, because time sits on Zinkoff's hands like an elephant. He hates to wait. He hates waiting more than anything else.

To Zinkoff, waiting means basically this: not moving. He hates waiting in lines. He hates waiting for the bathroom to clear out. He hates waiting for answers, for toast to pop up, for bathtubs to fill, for soup to heat, soup to cool, car rides to end.

Most of all he hates sleep, the curse of the human race. Every night he protests it, every morning he gets out of it as soon as he can. In fact, as far as Zinkoff is concerned, he doesn't really sleep. He merely waits all night until it's time to get up. If pressed, he will admit to going to bed, but not to sleep.

Relatives and other grown-ups have discovered that they can amuse themselves by asking him, "So Donald, when did you go to bed last night?"

"Nine o'clock."

"And when did you go to sleep?"

"I didn't."

"You mean you didn't sleep all night?"

"Nope."

Whenever his uncle Stanley comes over, he

proclaims at full voice: "Aha—there he is! The Sleepless Wonder!"

Then there are the sitting things: watching movies and reading books and the hours in the classroom. Like sleeping, these too are non-movers—but not entirely. For as long as they keep his interest, as long as they make him think, Zinkoff is moving. Of course, you wouldn't know it to look at him, since the moving part is out of sight, behind his unblinking eyes. His brain.

This is how Zinkoff at the age of eight imagines the inside of his head: a moving part, like an elbow or knee. He imagines that when he's interested, when he's thinking, his brain is moving, stretching itself, leaning this way and that, flexing. When his brain stops moving—that is, when he's bored—off goes the TV, closed goes the book, tuned out goes the teacher.

Zinkoff's blessing has been this: Boredom has not happened often.

But it happens a lot during his three weeks of convalescing. Every day he looks out the front window at the kids going off to John W. Satterfield

Elementary. Not only is he not allowed to go to school, he is forbidden to do anything more active than walk across a room. His world shrinks to the living-room sofa. He soon becomes fed up with TV and books. Fed up with jigsaw puzzles and watercolors. Fed up with feeling the stitches of his operation. Minute after minute, day after endless day he stares out the front window, and the elephant lowers itself onto his hands, and he comes to know the Long Wait of the Waiting Man.

He comes to know how painful a minute can be, how unbearable an hour. Though he cannot put his understanding into words, he understands that time by itself is nothing, is emptiness, and that a person is not made for emptiness. One day he counts as thirty-two minutes go by on the clock, and he says to himself as he looks out the window, "Thirty-two years." He tries to cast his brain, like a stone, that far, thirty-two years into the future, but all it falls into is an immense gray sadness. He knows it is not his own sadness but the sadness of the Waiting Man. It is everywhere, on the roof shingles and rainspouts and brick walls and alleyways, and the sadness and the emptiness are the same thing and they will not end until a soldier comes walking down Willow Street.

Zinkoff turns from the window. He feels an urgent need to play with his baby sister. He plays with her for an hour or two and makes her laugh, and then, because still he cannot go to school, he decides that school must come to him.

He will give himself a test.

14 · The Furnace Monster

To Zinkoff there is not one darkness, but many. There is the dark in the closet and the dark under the bed and the dark he can never see: the dark inside a drawer. No matter how fast he opens a drawer, trying to catch the dark, the light pours in faster. There is the dark of outside and the dark of inside.

Unlike most children, Zinkoff is not afraid of the dark. Outside darkness does not frighten him. His father has told him that the stars are faraway suns, and the thought of all those suns up there gives Zinkoff a warm and cozy feeling at night. Inside, he seems to carry his own sunshine with him—he's a sunshine bottle—even into the closet, where sometimes he hides from Polly without a twinge of fear.

In one respect, however, he is like almost all

children: He fears the darkness of the cellar. And even then, it isn't strictly the darkness that he fears. It's what dwells in the darkness: the Furnace Monster.

Like most furnace monsters, Zinkoff's stays out of sight behind the furnace when people are around. It's when the people leave, when the light goes off and the door at the top of the stairs closes, in that purest darkness—that's when the monster comes out from behind the furnace.

To be in the cellar then, this is the most terrifying thing Zinkoff can imagine. This will be his test.

Perhaps if Zinkoff had not had two weeks to build up a good head of boredom, taking the test would not have occurred to him. But he is bored and it does occur to him and, for Zinkoff, that is that: If it occurs to him, he does it.

One day while his mother is on the phone and Polly is napping, he opens the door in the kitchen and stands at the head of the cellar stairs. He turns on the light. The cellar appears dimly below him, lit only by a bare forty-watt bulb. He counts the number of steps. There are nine. To his eyes they look like nine hundred. Nine hundred steps into a bottomless black hole.

Knees trembling, one sweaty hand on the railing, the other flat against the wall, he lowers himself one step. He's breathing fast, as if he's been running. He sits down.

He sits for a long time. He has thought that after a while he would begin to feel better, but he doesn't. He doesn't want to lower himself one more inch. He wants only one thing in this world, to turn around, take one step back up, turn out the light, reenter the kitchen, close the door, and go curl up with Polly. He imagines himself doing exactly that . . .

. . . and lowers himself down to the next step.

More of the cellar comes into view: the cold, gray, cracked concrete floor; the once white-washed walls, now gray and streaked with green slime, gashed and oozing sand; the coarse, time-worn planks of his father's workbench. The modern geometry of the oil furnace and water heater seem out of place in this crumbling pit that reminds Zinkoff of ancient ruins.

He lowers himself another step . . . and thinks he glimpses the furry edge of a flank pulling itself out of sight.

He grips the front edge of the step with both hands. He stares bug-eyed into the shadows.

The Monster speaks.

Zinkoff bolts. Back up the stairs and into the kitchen, into its glorious familiar light, the stitches in his stomach tingling. He knows it wasn't really the Monster. It was really the oil furnace kicking on with a *whoosh*. He knows it, he knows it. Nevertheless he doesn't go near the cellar door.

Until the next day.

The next day he goes down three more steps. He is truly down into the cellar now, closer to the gray stone floor than to the top of the stairs. He looks back up at the light from the kitchen. He repeats to himself: "It's only a cellar. It's only a cellar." His heart is banging to get out. His stitches tingle. Beyond the hum of the furnace he can hear his mother's voice. She is on the phone a lot these days. She has gotten a job as a tele-marketer. She sells memberships to a health club over the phone. He whispers in the direction of the furnace: "Please don't come out."

There is one other sound: the *tock-tock* of his mother's cooking timer. He has set it at five minutes and brought it with him. It sits on the step beside him. It sounds like the thunder of a kettle drum. He has just decided the timer is broken when it goes off with a firebell clang. He yelps. Back to the kitchen.

On the third day he leaves the timer behind. He lowers himself step by step until his feet rest on the cold cellar floor. He starts counting, whispering the numbers. He will stay until he reaches one hundred. It is noticeably cooler down here. Above him a slurry of light barely leaks from the forty-watt bulb, mocking the sun and stars he loves. A smear of light puddles at the far corner of the furnace. At last he reaches one hundred and returns to the kitchen.

He tries to feel good, to congratulate himself for what he has accomplished. But he cannot fool himself. He cannot forget that the test is not over.

The next day he returns to the doctor's office

to get his stitches out. Then comes the weekend. He resumes the test on Monday. He does the same thing he did the first day—he lowers himself down three steps—only this time there is one difference: He does not turn on the light. This time the only light reaching the cellar comes from the doorway at the top of the stairs. He begins counting.

How he wishes for the puny light from the forty-watt bulb! He holds up his hand. He stares at the backs of his fingers, anchors himself to the sight of them. His stitches are gone now, but the scar they left behind tingles on. By the time he reaches one hundred, the fingers he's staring at are shaking. He clambers up the stairs.

Next day: down six steps. More than halfway. The hand before his face less clear now. He finds himself counting too fast, makes himself slow down. It takes forever to reach one hundred.

When he descends to the bottom step next day, the hand he holds up is pale and ghostly. It does not seem to be his. He forces himself to stare into the blackness before him. He counts a new way: "The light is right behind me, five . . . the light is right behind me, ten . . . the light is right behind me, fifteen . . ." Some of the counts come out as burps. He burps a lot since the operation. By the end he's screaming, "The light is right behind me one hundred!" as he flies up the stairs.

His mother comes running. "What happened?"

"Nothing," he says.

"Why were you screaming? Why are you breathing so hard?"

"I am?"

She takes his chin in her hand and tilts his face upward. "I think we'll both be glad when you go back to school. Back to the sofa."

As usual Zinkoff is first up next morning. He is so nervous, he's burping even more than usual. He can hardly get his breakfast down. Hard as the darkness test has been so far, the worst is yet to come. He waits for his father to leave for work. He waits for his mother to begin her tele-marketing phone calls. He peers into the living room—The Alarm is in her playpen, guarding the front door.

For a long time he sits alone in the kitchen, feeling the light, soaking it up, imagining himself a light sponge. Never before has he so appreciated the mere sight of common things. The silvery sides of the toaster and its tiny pinched reflections. The plump blue-and-yellow Dutch boy cookie jar. The red straw sticking up from Polly's drinking cup.

He takes one last look around. Will he ever see these things again?

He pulls from his pocket the single sock that he has brought along. He bunches it into a ball and sticks it into his mouth. He sits some more.

He ponders his plan: three steps on the first day, three more on the second, down to the bottom on the third.

At last he pushes himself up from the chair and, like a condemned man, takes the long, doomed walk to the cellar door.

He opens the door. He takes one step forward. He pulls the door shut behind him.

And learns that his fear has missed the target.

He was expecting darkness, yes, really dark darkness—but this is something else. This is darkness so absolute, so wickedly pure that he himself seems to have been wiped out. He holds his hand one inch before his face and cannot—positively can not—see it. He reaches for his opposite forearm, missing it on the first try, to reassure himself that he is still there. He squeezes the forearm in hopes that some of the light he has sponged up will come squirting out. It does not.

He reaches behind for the door, for its smooth painted surface. His trembling fingers find the doorknob. *Turn it*, a voice inside his ear whispers, *turn it and go back*. And that's what he tells his hand, *turn it*, but his hand is not listening, his hand is letting go and now his whole body, contrary to all his wishes and good sense, is lowering itself to a seat on the first step.

And he learns a second thing: He can forget the three-day plan. He must do it all today.

Now.

Or never.

He lowers himself one more step, seven to go . . . one more step, six to go . . . one more . . . one more . . . his silent scream probes for a weakness in the sock . . . one more . . . one more . . . and the Monster is out from behind the furnace now, he knows it, he feels it. The Monster is in front of the furnace and is moving toward the stairway. The Monster is inches in front of his face now, he can touch it if he reaches out . . . or takes one more step . . .

. . . the scar is singing . . .

He doesn't think about it, he just does it. Two steps from the bottom he turns and runs back up the stairs.

In the dazzling light of the kitchen he rips the sock from his mouth. He stands gasping over a chair. He thinks of the two steps he stopped short of. He has failed. Flunked his own test. He thinks about it for several moments. He hears his mother's voice on the phone, upstairs. He listens. He heads off to play with Polly.

Four days later he goes back to school.

15 · Discovered

In fourth grade Zinkoff is discovered.

He has been there all along, of course, in the neighborhood, in the school, for ten years. He is already known as the kid who laughs too much and, until his operation, the kid who throws up. In fact, in order to get himself discovered, Zinkoff does not do a single thing he hasn't already done a thousand times.

As with all discoveries, it is the eye and not the object that changes.

The discovery of Zinkoff, which will take place gradually over the course of the year, begins on the first day of school. The teacher is Mr. Yalowitz. He is the class's first man teacher. Mr. Yalowitz stands up front holding the stack of roll cards. He looks carefully at each card, as if he is memorizing every name. Then he begins to shuffle the cards, rearranging their places in the stack. When he finishes he puts the stack down. He lifts off the top card. "Zinkoff," he says, his eyes never leaving the card. "Donald Zinkoff. Where are you?"

Zinkoff, knowing by now where he belongs, has already gone straight to the boondocks: last seat, far corner. He jumps to attention. "Here, sir!" he calls out.

A smile crosses the teacher's face. He looks up. "Zinkoff . . . Zinkoff . . . You want to know something, Zinkoff?"

"Yes, sir!"

"You're the first Z I've ever had in my class. It's not easy being a Z, is it, Zzzzinkoff?"

To tell the truth, Zinkoff has never thought much about it. "I don't know, sir."

"Well, it's *not* easy, take my word for it. I was a Y. Always the last seat in the class. Always the last one in line for this or that. Doomed by the alphabet. What do you think about that, Zinkoff?"

Zinkoff doesn't know what to think about

that, and he says so. As for the rest of the class, they're thinking, *So this is fourth grade*. They don't know if it's being one more grade up, or if it's this man teacher with his gruff man way of talking, but they're liking it and starting to feel pretty puffy about themselves.

The teacher points. "Zinkoff, how'd you like to experience life in the first row?"

Zinkoff's eyes boggle.

The teacher waves grandly. "Come on up here, boy!"

Zinkoff cries out "Yahoo!" and races up front.

By the time the teacher is done, Zinkoff is in seat number one and Rachel Abano is in the boondocks. Joining Zinkoff on the front row are a W, a V and two T's.

Thanks to teacher Yalowitz, the first person to discover Zinkoff is Zinkoff. Unlike his teachers in grades two and three, this one seems delighted with him. He is forever making pronouncements that give Zinkoff new views of himself. Every morning the first week, for example, as soon as Zinkoff enters the classroom, the teacher proclaims, "And the Z shall be first!"

One day as he arrives for work at 7:30 A.M., the teacher spots Zinkoff, alone on the playground, coming down the sliding board. He calls out, "You'll be early to your own funeral, boy!"

Like Zinkoff's previous teachers, Mr. Yalowitz notes his atrocious handwriting. "Master Z," he says, "whenever you put pencil to paper, unspeakable things happen." Unlike the other teachers, he says this while laughing, and adds, "Thank God for keyboards!"

Mr. Yalowitz is fussy about his greenboard. Every Friday at precisely two thirty in the afternoon he washes his greenboard. For this purpose he keeps a bucket and sponge in the book-and-supply closet.

On a Friday afternoon in November Mr. Yalowitz is called away from class. By the time he gets back it is well past two thirty. Zinkoff is up front, standing on a chair, reaching for the highest part of the greenboard with the wet sponge.

Mr. Yalowitz gives a chuckle. "Independent little critter, aren't you?"

Zinkoff isn't sure if his teacher's remark is a statement or a question, nor does he quite understand what it means. But he likes the sound of it and decides it must be good, whatever it is. He looks down at the teacher and beams. "Yes sir!"

The teacher makes himself comfortable while his student finishes the job. When Zinkoff returns to his front-row seat, the class applauds. Someone even whistles.

By placing Zinkoff up front, by spotlighting Zinkoff with clever remarks, Mr. Yalowitz unwittingly hastens the others' discovery of him. Something else hastens that discovery too: new eyes.

By the end of third grade, most of the kids' baby teeth were gone. The permanent ones had arrived in their mouths. Around fourth grade something similar happens with eyes. The baby eyes don't drop out, nor are there eye fairies around to leave quarters under pillows, but new eyes do arrive nevertheless. Big-kid eyes replace little-kid eyes.

Little-kid eyes are scoopers. They just scoop

up everything they see and swallow it whole, no questions asked. Big-kid eyes are picky. They notice things that the little-kid eyes never bothered with: the way a teacher blows her nose, the way a kid dresses or pronounces a word.

Twenty-seven classmates now turn their new big-kid eyes to Zinkoff, and suddenly they see things they haven't seen before. Zinkoff has always been clumsy, but now they notice. Zinkoff has always been messy and atrocious and too early and giggly and slow and more often than not wrong in his answers. But now they notice. They notice the stars on his shirts and his atrocious hair and his atrocious way of walking and the atrocious way he volunteers for everything. They notice it all. Even the dime-sized birthmark on his neck below his right earlobe. It has been there for ten years, but now they notice and they stare and say, "What's *that*?"

When the teacher returns graded papers, they peek over Zinkoff's shoulder and see that he never gets an A. When the music teacher comes and demonstrates instruments and passes out sheets to sign up for lessons and orchestra, they peek again and see that the silly goose signed up for all eight instruments.

Those who practice with him in the school orchestra notice that he is given the "thunder drum," as the teacher calls it. They notice that every time he pounds the drum he is three beats early or three beats late, and they wince and roll their big-kid eyes at each other and scowl at the teacher as if to say, *Do something.*

And she does something. She gives him a flute, the least damaging instrument. Still he often veers off course, a wanderer among the clarinets and violins. The orchestra kids tell the rest of the kids, the rest of the kids tell their parents, and when the chorus and orchestra recital takes place that spring nearly everyone in the audience keeps an ear peeled for the lost, solitary squeak of Zinkoff's flute.

It is in the first week of June of that year that Zinkoff is most profoundly discovered. It happens during Field Day.

16 · Field Day

Field Day is many years old at Satterfield Elementary. It began as a day of fun. A day to celebrate spring. An outdoor treat for the students.

And Field Day still is fun for the little kids, the first-, second- and third-graders. But for the fourth- and fifth-graders, the big kids, it is less about fun and more about winning and losing.

The little kids take part in events designed just for them: the potato roll, kick the pillow, basketball boomerang, shadow bonkers. For the big kids it's races. Ten kinds of races, all of them relays. There's the sack race and the run-backwards race and the hop-on-one-foot race and the race-backwards-while-sitting-on-your-rear-end race. The first nine races are like that: goofy, unusual. The last race is just a plain race. To the big, fast kids, it is the only real race.

Each classroom is divided into four teams—eight teams per grade. Each team has a color. Students compete only against those in their own grade.

Mr. Yalowitz is the coach. From home he has brought in strips of dyed material: headbands. Team colors for his classroom are purple, red, green and yellow. Zinkoff is on the purple team.

Before they go out for Field Day Mr. Yalowitz gathers his students around him and says, "I'm rooting for all you guys. Reds, Greens, Purples, Yellows. It's those other fourth-grade measles I don't like." The kids laugh. He's always telling them that they are better than the other fourth-grade class and that they and their teacher, Mrs. Serota, are measles. "So let's go out there today and beat the pants off 'em!"

They pile hands into the huddle and explode from the classroom and stampede shrieking down the hallway and into the sunshine of May.

The Purple team has seven members. The best athlete among them is a boy named Gary Hobin. Tall and long of leg, Hobin is not only the fastest Purple, he is probably the fastest kid in all of fourth grade. He is also a take-charge kind of kid, and when he says, "I'm leading off every race," none of the Purples disagree. But when Coach Yalowitz hears about it, he says, "Nobody runs every race. You rotate so everybody gets a chance."

Everybody does get a chance, but Zinkoff gets less of a chance than the others. He "runs" the second leg of the race-backwards-while-sitting-on-your-rear-end race—or, as the kids call it, the hiney hop—and is quickly left behind by the other seven teams. But Yolanda Perry and Gary Hobin are the final two legs, and they bring the Purples back to a rousing victory by a nose, so to speak.

In the hop-on-one-foot race, even an incredible final leg by Hobin is not enough to make up the ground lost by Zinkoff, whose two feet are not always enough to keep him upright. The sight of Zinkoff tilting, tottering, lurching, falling, brings howls of laughter and mock cheers from the sidelines.

Nevertheless, going into the final event the Purples have the highest point total of any fourth-grade team. To win the championship, all they have to do is not finish last in the big race. Naturally, six of the Purples have no intention of allowing Zinkoff to compete. And naturally, Gary Hobin will run the most important leg, the last leg—the anchor leg—and will propel the Purples to glory.

But the coach has other ideas.

"Zinkoff runs anchor," he says to the seven gathered Purples.

Everyone turns to stare at Zinkoff, who is doing jumping jacks to keep in shape.

Gary Hobin squawks, *"What?"*

"You run third leg," says the coach. "Give him a nice lead." And off he goes to counsel the Reds, Greens and Yellows.

Six Purples glare at Zinkoff. Gary Hobin balls his fist and holds it an inch from Zinkoff's face. "I'm gonna give you the biggest lead anybody ever saw. You better not lose it."

"I won't lose it," says Zinkoff. "I always save my best till last."

Which in fact is not true at all, but Zinkoff

imagines it to be, and it sounds like a good thing to say at the time.

The big final race is run across the length of the playground, through the yellow dust and tufted grass. The starters for the eight fourth-grade teams line up at the sliding board and take off at the principal's "Go!" The second runners crouch at the far end, waiting to be tagged on the back by the leadoffs.

At the first exchange the Purples are in second place. By the time the second runner tags Hobin, they are five yards ahead. Hobin blasts out of his crouch and spins dust like a yellow tornado. True to his word, Hobin gives Zinkoff such a lead as has not been seen all day. When he tags Zinkoff, the other runners are only halfway down the track. "Go!" Hobin yells, and Zinkoff goes.

Zinkoff's legs churn up the dust. His arms whirl like his mother's Mixmaster. His face is a pinched, grimacing lemon of effort. And yet—somehow—he goes nowhere. When the other anchors take off he is barely ten yards down the track. "Run! Run!" Hobin screams behind him.

Unable to contain himself, Hobin leaves his place and runs up alongside Zinkoff and screams in his ear, "Run, you dumb turtle! Run!"

Zinkoff runs and runs, the flap of his headband bobbing behind like a tiny purple tail, and he is still running long after the others have crossed the finish line. Zinkoff comes in dead last. The Purples come in last. The Purples lose the championship.

The Purples tear off their headbands. They slam them to the ground, stomp them into the yellow dust. Zinkoff is bent over, gasping from his great effort, catching his breath. Hobin comes to him. He kicks dust over Zinkoff's sneakers. Zinkoff looks up. Hobin sneers, "You're a loser. A stinkin' loser."

Other Purples pile on.

"Yeah. You stink at *everything*. Why do you even *do* stuff?"

"Yeah. Why do you even get outta *bed* in the morning?"

"He prolly even screws *that* up!"

One Purple shakes his fist. "We coulda had *medals*!"

They file by. Some whisper the word. Some say it aloud. Each pronounces it perfectly.

"Loser."

"Loser."

"Loser."

"Loser."

"Loser."

He hopes his parents won't ask him about Field Day at dinner, but they do. They say, "How'd it go?"

"How'd what go?" he says.

"Field Day."

"Oh, okay." Trying to sound like it's not worth talking about. Don't ask who won, he prays.

And they don't. They ask: "Was it fun?" and "What was your favorite race?" and "Did you get all sweaty?"

And he thinks he's out of the woods when Polly pipes up: "Didja win?"

He screams at her. "No! Okay?"

And everybody stops chewing and stares and he runs from the dinner table crying. He half expects his father to follow him up to his room, but he doesn't. Instead, he calls up: "Hey, want to go for a ride?" Zinkoff is always asking to go for a ride, and his father always says not unless there's someplace particular to go, or it's a waste of gas.

Zinkoff doesn't need to be asked twice. He flies downstairs and off they go in Clunker Six. There's some chitchat in the car, but most of it goes from his father to the jittery dashboard. "Easy there, honeybug . . . no big deal . . . I'm right here . . ." The rest is just a ride to no place in particular, wasting gas galore.

Even in bed that night Zinkoff can still feel the shake and shimmy of the old rattletrap, and coming through loud and clear is a message that was never said. He knows that he could lose a thousand races and his father will never give up on him. He knows that if he ever springs a leak or throws a gasket, his dad will be there with duct tape and chewing gum to patch him up, that no matter how much he rattles and knocks, he'll always be a honeybug to his dad, never a clunker.

17 · **What the Clocks Say**

At Satterfield Elementary you can't go any higher than fifth grade, so fifth-graders rule the school. When other students look at you, most of what they see is bigger and better. You know more. You eat more. You draw better. You sing better. You throw farther and run faster. You go to the head of the line. You drink longest at the water fountains. You even talk louder and laugh harder.

If you have made it through the first four grades, fifth grade is your reward. The payoff. And it comes in ways that aren't even visible. It comes as a feeling whenever you are in the presence of kids from the lower grades, a feeling, even though nobody says it, that you are the most important. Fifth grade is a great time to be alive.

All of this greets Zinkoff when he returns to

school, and he loves it. He loves being a fifth-grader.

Something else is there too. It has been growing through the summer after taking root in the yellow dust of the playground. It has invaded the school building and multiplied abundantly. As Zinkoff's classmates return in September, many of them pick it up along with their new pencils and other school supplies.

It is the word. It is Zinkoff's new name. It is not in the roll book.

Rarely does anyone say his new name to his face, but it is often said behind a giggle or a cough. It comes from here, from there. Zinkoff sometimes senses someone being called, but the sound of it is not the sound of his name as he knows it, so he does not turn.

And then one day, for no good reason, hearing the name, he does turn. But no one is looking at him, so he thinks he must be mistaken. And the voices continue, and again he turns, and again. But no one is ever looking, no one ever seems to have spoken. It is as if the voices are coming from the walls and the clocks and the lights in the ceiling.

Loser.

The discovery and renaming of Zinkoff is a great convenience to the student body. Zinkoff has been tagged and bagged, and now virtually everything he does can be dumped into the same sack. His sloppy handwriting and artwork, his hapless fluting, his mediocre grades, his clumsiness, his birthmark—everything is seen as an extension of his performance on Field Day, everything is seen as a matter of losing. It is as if he loses a hundred races every day.

But except for the voices of the clocks, Zinkoff is unaware of all this. He is too busy thinking about himself to notice what others are thinking. He is busy growing up. He is busy growing out.

By the start of fifth grade Zinkoff has grown out of a whole flock of beliefs: Santa Claus, the Easter Bunny, the Tooth Fairy, rabbits' feet, talking dinosaurs, the Man in the Moon, unicorns, gremlins, dragons, sidewalk cracks. Though he is still scared stiff of the dark in the cellar, he no longer believes in the Furnace Monster. Beliefs are just flying off him. Thus unweighted, he can feel himself growing taller.

He no longer wears paper stars on his shirts, though he does continue to accept congratulations. He replaces his little-kid giggle with a big-kid laugh, which he works on in his bedroom—to the annoyance of Polly, who thinks she is always missing something funny. He no longer yells "Yahoo!" (But he still wants to be a mailman, and he still says his prayers at night.) He admits to sleeping.

He tries to outgrow being clumsy, but it doesn't work. His handwriting is still atrocious, but only to others, not to himself, so he doesn't worry about it.

One Saturday his mother has a yard sale. She asks him if he minds her selling some of his old toys, the ones Polly has no use for. "No problem," he says. Then she brings out his old giraffe hat. Would he mind her selling this? He looks at it. Faded, fuzzworn. Hasn't seen it in years.

Whatever once possessed him to put that silly thing on his head? "No problem," he says, and feels himself pop up another half inch.

He loves growing up, loves feeling himself take up more space in this world.

He is allowed to go farther from home now. He has a bike, a secondhand yard sale two-wheeler with a junior rattle of its own that reminds him of his father's car, so he calls it Clinker One. He loves it. He's allowed to ride it almost anywhere in town, as long as he stays on the sidewalks and walks it across streets. Sometimes he obeys, sometimes not.

His favorite place to go is the nine hundred block of Willow Street, where he delivered the mail on Take Zinkoff to Work Day when he was seven. The Waiting Man is still there, at the window, staring up the street, his hair longer about the ears, missing more on top. One thing Zinkoff has definitely not outgrown is thinking about the Waiting Man. Sometimes he parks his bike and walks up the street so the Waiting Man will be looking right at him. But even then the Waiting

Man doesn't seem to see him. Sometimes he stands under the window, hoping the Waiting Man will turn his head, at least that. But he never does.

So fierce is the Waiting Man's concentration, so endless his patience that Zinkoff half expects the missing-in-action brother to burst into existence one day right there on the sidewalk. Twice, in fact, he dreams that a soldier toting a rifle on his shoulder is walking toward him. The longer the soldier does not really appear, the worse Zinkoff feels for the brother in the window. He cannot believe the world will allow such waiting and wanting to go unrewarded.

For several excited days he has an idea. He will dress himself in camouflage pants and shirt, pull on some boots and find an old rifle or BB gun somewhere and go walking up Willow Street—just to give the man a moment or two of happiness. But he soon realizes that would be cruel, and he ditches the whole idea.

Sometimes as he pedals up the nine hundred block the lady with the walker is there on her top step. Whenever she spots him she calls,

"Mailman! Oh, mailman!" After a while he always makes sure he has a letter for her, a little note that says "Hi, how are you?" or "I hope you are feeling well." He's older now, so his letters don't have to be nonsense.

And now there is someone new, a little girl. Her brown hair is always gathered in a puppy tail with a yellow band. Apparently she has only recently learned to walk, because she lurches when she takes a step and her little dumpling knees wobble. She can never get far, however, as she is attached to a leash.

The leash is a length of clothesline. One end is hooked to a harness which the little girl wears like a strap jacket. Sometimes the other end is tied around an ancient bootscrape, sometimes it's in the hand of the little girl's mother, who in warm weather sits on the front steps reading a book.

"I never saw a person with a leash on," Zinkoff says one day, curiosity drawing him and his bike to the curb. He's thinking how he would have hated a leash.

The mother looks up from her book and gives

him a fine smile. "I never did either," she says. "I lived on a farm and all my mother had to worry about was me being run over by a chicken."

Zinkoff laughs. "Does she like it?"

The mother looks at her daughter. "I don't think she likes or dislikes it. Yet, anyway. As far as she's concerned, this is just the way life is. First you crawl, then you get a leash. If she starts to complain, I guess we'll have to have a chat."

"She talks?" says Zinkoff.

The mother laughs. "About three words. That's why I win all the arguments. So far."

Whenever they are out front, Zinkoff stops his bike to say hello. He finds out that the little girl's name is Claudia. After a while, Claudia begins to recognize him. She totters out to meet him at the curb, the leash's limit. She seems to be a giving person. She always reaches down into the gutter and picks up something—a pebble, discarded chewing gum—and holds it out to him. It's always dirty, her mother always scolds her, and Zinkoff, not wanting to be ungrateful, always says a formal "thank you" to Claudia and pockets the gift.

On days when he doesn't cruise nine hundred Willow he often rides to Halftank Hill. Halftank Hill is in the park and the best part of it is a grassy, evilly steep slope that commands: *Come down me!* And they do, kids from all over town, in all seasons of the year. They sled down, they run down, roll down, tumble down, bicycle down, tricycle down, Rollerblade down, skateboard down, trashcan-lid down.

Early in his life, when Zinkoff raced cars along the sidewalk, he had believed himself to be the fastest kid in the world. Now that he knows this to be untrue, Halftank Hill has become all the more appealing to him.

Sometimes he runs, because it is the only way he can experience, for just a moment, a particularly fascinating feeling. Halfway down the hill he can feel himself losing control, his legs cannot keep up with his speed. He feels as if he is coming apart, running out of himself, leaving himself behind.

Sometimes he bikes it. He aims the front tire over the grassy crest and down he goes, and for those few seconds nothing can convince him that he is not the fastest thing in the universe, and even though he's too big now to yell yahoo he yells it anyway: "Yahoo!" And rediscovers every time that no one is slow on Halftank Hill. And there are no clocks.

Sometimes he doesn't want to ride anywhere in particular. Sometimes he doesn't want to ride fast. He just wants to ride. That's when he aims Clinker One for the alleys, where cats and little kids roam but no cars, a bicycle's boulevard, and he rides, just rides, and it's good enough.

And so Zinkoff's life in fifth grade is filled with things new and interesting and good enough. And until the day of the test-that-is-not-a-test, it never occurs to him that something has been missing.

18 · Best Friend

It isn't a schoolwork test. There has been nothing to study for. There has been no warning. One day in fifth grade the teacher, Mrs. Shankfelder, simply passes out booklets with blue covers. Barry Peterson says, "Is this a test?" and she says no, she calls it some big word. But Zinkoff looks at it and sees that there are questions and there are little egg spaces to fill in for answers. It's a test.

Every other school test Zinkoff has ever taken has been about some classroom subject: arithmetic, geography, spelling. This test seems to be about himself. What does he think about this? Why does he do that? Which one of these does he prefer?

Halfway through, Zinkoff has to admit this is the first test he has ever taken that is almost fun. It's one more thing this year that makes him feel grown-up. Most of the answers come easily to him, until on the next-to-last page he arrives at a question that stumps him:

Who is your best friend?

Unlike most of the other questions, this one isn't multiple choice. No little eggs to fill in, just a blank line that needs a name.

If he had this test back in second grade, he would have filled in Andrew Orwell's name. But Andrew, his neighbor, has long since moved, and no obvious replacement comes to mind.

Oh sure, Zinkoff has friends. There's Bucky Monastra, who he plays marbles with. And Peter Grilot, the second sloppiest kid in class. And Katie Snelsen, who smiles at him every time she sees him. Friends all, but not best friends.

He knows what a best friend is. He sees them all over. Best friends are Burt O'Neill and George Undercoffler. Or Ellen Dabney and Ronni Jo Thomas. Best friends are always together, always whispering and laughing and running, always at each other's house, having dinner, sleeping over. They are practically adopted by each other's parents. You can't pry them apart.

Zinkoff doesn't have anybody like that. Most

of the time he doesn't think about it. But now and then he does. He wonders what it would be like to be so stuck to another kid that you could walk into his kitchen and his mother wouldn't even look up because she's that used to you, and she would say, "Wash your hands and sit down, you're late for dinner." It seems kind of neat, thinking of it that way, and sometimes he regrets he doesn't have a best friend. But then he usually thinks about his own mother and his father and Polly and he thinks about the nine hundred block of Willow and he figures he is doing okay.

Until he comes to this question—*Who is your best friend?*—and that blank space seems to be saying to him: *If you don't have one, you'd better get one.*

He skips over the question to finish the rest of the test. He returns to it. Time is passing. Pretty soon Mrs. Shankfelder will say, "Pencils up."

Best friend . . . best friend . . .

"One more minute," says Mrs. Shankfelder, who does not usually give a warning.

He panics. He looks around the classroom, too bad if the teacher thinks he's cheating. His eye settles on Hector Binns, way up in the first row. Hector's head is down, his shoulders hunched. He's working away on the test.

Hector Binns has been in Zinkoff's class since first grade, so of course Zinkoff knows who he is. Over the years they have found themselves at the same water fountain or monkey bar rung. But Hector Binns, being a B, has always sat far from Zinkoff, and Zinkoff's information about him is spotty at best. This is the sum of what he knows: Hector Binns wears glasses, he is about Zinkoff's height, he loves black licorice and he's always cleaning out his ear with a paper clip. And now that he thinks of it, there's one more thing: As far as Zinkoff knows, Hector Binns is available. He has no best friend either.

"Pencils up."

Quickly he fills in the blank, misspelling both first and last names: "Hecter Binz."

He can hardly wait for recess. He finds Hector Binns by the bicycle rack, working on his ear with a paper clip.

"Hi, Hector," he says. "What's up?"

"Huh?" replies Hector Binns. Zinkoff repeats,

"What's up?" but Hector doesn't seem to hear. Maybe his hearing goes bad when the paper clip is in his ear. Otherwise, he doesn't seem unfriendly, so Zinkoff just stands there.

Binns goes at his ear with a gusto that Zinkoff has never noticed before. He digs and scrapes, wincing in pain or pleasure, Zinkoff can't tell which. He pulls out the paper clip and examines it. To Zinkoff's eye it's clean. Binns plunges it into the other ear. Dig, scrape, wince. This time the clip comes out with a tiny waxy orangish crumb clinging to the end of it.

Binns pulls from his pants pocket a small brown plastic bottle, the kind that pills come in. He brings the bottle to his mouth and for an instant Zinkoff thinks he's going to eat it, but he simply pulls off the white flip-top cap with his teeth. He taps the paper clip on the rim of the bottle and in falls the waxy crumb. Zinkoff notices that the bottle is half full. Binns returns bottle and paper clip to his pocket. Only then does Binns seem to notice that he is not alone.

The obvious question crawls to the front of Zinkoff's tongue, but somehow he holds it back.

"So," he says, "who did you answer for best friend?"

Binns pulls out a pack of black licorice sticks from another pocket. He rips off half a stick and begins to chew. "Nobody," he says.

"Really?" says Zinkoff. "You left it blank? Can you do that?"

Binns shakes his head. Except for that first moment, his eyes never meet Zinkoff's. He always seems to be looking into the Beyond. "I wrote Nobody. The word Nobody."

"Oh," says Zinkoff, nodding, thinking he understands. "Nobody. Okay."

Binns stuffs the rest of the stick into his mouth and returns the pack to his pocket. "Nobody is my lizard."

Zinkoff stares at the eyes that stare at the Beyond. Suddenly he gets it. "Oh! You have a lizard named Nobody."

Binns blinks, which Zinkoff takes for a nod.

"And you put him down as your best friend." Another blink. "Okay, I got it."

Hector Binns collects earwax and has a lizard named Nobody, who he calls his best friend.

Zinkoff figures his choice is looking better by the minute.

"Know who I put down?" he says.

"No," says Binns.

"You," says Zinkoff.

Binns blinks. His eyes disconnect from the Beyond and slide over to Zinkoff's face. "Huh?" he says.

Zinkoff grins. "Yeah. I put your name down."

Binns's eyelids flap as if they're trying to take off. "Me? Why?"

"Because I had to put *somebody's* name down, and I thought of you."

"But I'm not your best friend."

"I know. And I'm not yours either. But I thought maybe we *could* be, I mean, since I wrote your name down and all."

Hector Binns isn't answering. His eyes have gone back to the Beyond.

Zinkoff doesn't know the word negotiation, but that's what this is. He tries to think of something he can offer, something to sweeten the pot. "I make a mean snickerdoodle cookie!" he blurts.

Binns's left cheek bulges out as he chews on his

licorice wad. When his teeth appear, they're out-
lined in black, as if cartoon-drawn. As a fifth-
grader, Zinkoff knows cool when he sees it. He
takes a stab at cool himself. He shuffles his feet.
He hooks his thumbs into his waistband. He gazes
off into a Beyond of his own. "So," he says, tossing in a shrug, "what do you think?" Making it
sound like, "Not that I care one way or the other."

Binns sniffs. He turns his head until he's looking down over his right shoulder. His lips slide to
the side of his face, the far corner of his mouth
opens like a little eye and out comes a black dol-
lop of licorice juice. It falls to the ground. At last
he speaks, and answers Zinkoff's held-back question. "What I think is, when I get enough wax
I'm gonna make a candle."

Wow! An earwax candle! Zinkoff is willing to
bet that Binns has not shared this blockbuster
information with anyone else in class.

The end-of-recess bell rings. The two of
them trot side by side to the door. "See ya after
school?" says Zinkoff.

Binns says, "I guess."

19 · The Candy in His Hand

At dinner that day he says at the table, says it casually to show it's an everyday thing, "I'll be going over to my best friend's house one of these days." Hoping his parents will take the bait and ask him who his best friend is.

They do. His mother's eyebrows go up. "Oh?" she says, "And who would that be?"

"Hector Binns," he replies, tossing it out casually, being cool, liking the sound of it.

"Isn't he in your class?"

"Yeah. He sits in the front row. He loves licorice."

"Loves it, huh?" says his father.

"Yeah."

"I hate licorice," says Polly. "Licorice smells."

"He's making a candle," he tells them.

"That's nice," says his mother.

"Out of earwax."

Everyone stops eating and stares at him.

"Earwax?" says his mother.

"Eewwwww!" goes Polly.

"Is that possible?" says his father.

Zinkoff feels a surge of associated pride. He looks his dad in the eye. "He's doing it."

Several days later he visits Hector Binns's house. He walks right in and plops himself down in a chair, because that's how you do it with a best friend: You walk right in and plop yourself down. When Binns's mother spots him her face goes all funny and she says, "Who are you?" But then Binns himself comes in and takes him off to his room.

They spend some time looking at Binns's stuff. He meets Nobody the lizard. Then Binns tells him to wait in the hallway and closes the bedroom door. When he opens it, he holds in his hand a brown pill bottle already filled with earwax. "This is the first one," he says. "I keep it hid."

Zinkoff can't believe he's being allowed to see it. He feels truly honored.

Riding home that day on his bicycle, Zinkoff notices the marks dotting the sidewalks. Black licorice spit marks. He smiles.

Zinkoff is determined to be the best best friend he can be.

One day Barry Peterson calls Binns "Heckie." Zinkoff knows Binns hates being called that, so he says to Peterson, "Hey, that's not his name, it's Hector." Because that's what you do, you stand up for your best friend.

And you eat lunch with him and talk with him and share secrets and laugh a lot and go places and do stuff, and when you wake up in the morning, he's the first person you think of.

Zinkoff does all of this, and more. He starts eating black licorice. He pretends it's chewing tobacco. He walks around with a chaw bulging from his cheek. He tries spitting pretend tobacco juice, but his mother puts a quick stop to that.

Binns is probably the most interesting person Zinkoff knows, with the possible exception of the Waiting Man, and Zinkoff soon decides he needs to be interesting too. It's around that time that he discovers in one of his pockets a clump of petrified bubblegum. It's a gift from Claudia, the little leash-and-harness girl. It looks like a pink stone. He appoints it his lucky piece, which he will carry with him always and rub when he needs some luck. He feels more interesting already.

About a week into the best friendship, Zinkoff asks his mother if he can invite Binns to sleep over. She says sure. Excited, Zinkoff runs to the phone and calls Binns. Binns says, "I guess." Binns never says "yes." He always says "I guess."

But the sleepover has problems. Binns turns out to be a kicker and a roller. Actually, he's a regular bulldozer in bed. Zinkoff wakes up to find himself thumping to the floor. He climbs back into bed, and as soon as he gets to sleep it happens again. After the third time he takes the extra blanket from the closet and makes himself a bed on the floor.

Except for his bed, after that night, he shares everything he can with his best friend: the lunch in his paper bag (he has outgrown the lunch pail too), the allowance in his pocket, the candy in his hand, the joke in his giggle. He shares the nine hundred block of Willow with him. He introduces him to little Claudia on the leash. They walk their bikes past the Waiting Man. The lady with the walker isn't on the front step that day, so for days afterward Zinkoff keeps asking Binns if he wants to go back, because he wants Binns to hear her say, "Oh, mailman!" But Binns keeps saying, "I guess not."

There is one thing more special than any other that Zinkoff intends to share with Binns. He saves it for weeks and weeks, and when he can no longer bear to wait, he gives it to Binns. He gives it to him after school one day in a brown paper lunch bag. Binns opens the bag. In it is a little tin that says "Altoids." Zinkoff found the tin on the street. Binns opens the Altoids tin and stares.

"What is it?" he says.

Zinkoff beams. "Wax."

Binns stares, first at the contents of the tin, then at Zinkoff. That's all he does, stare.

"It's mine," says Zinkoff. "From my own ears.

I've been saving it up. I know it's not much, but I couldn't wait any longer. I figured you could add it to yours and get enough for a candle faster." He doesn't tell him that he tried to get Polly to contribute, but she refused.

Binns looks into the Beyond. He bends a licorice stick and stuffs it into his mouth. He slowly closes the lid of the Altoids tin and hands it back to Zinkoff. "I guess not," he says.

Zinkoff shrugs. "Okay." He understands. When a kid is making an earwax candle, he wants everything to come from his own ears. Zinkoff figures maybe he'll save up for a candle of his own. He wonders if that would count as a science project.

And then it's over.

20 · Nowhere

When is it over?

Zinkoff doesn't know for weeks. He is only dimly aware of things, dimly aware that as time goes by he seems to be seeing less and less of Binns. He rides to Binns's house and Binns isn't there. He phones. Binns says he has homework to do. He asks Binns this, asks him that. Binns always seems to say, "I guess not." Even Binns's voice over the phone seems to shrug, seems to be looking into the Beyond.

And then one spring day on the way to school Zinkoff sees a cluster of licorice spit marks on a sidewalk, and it makes him feel a little sad and remembery, and just like that he knows: It's over.

And something new begins.

On that same spring day something happens to Zinkoff. An A happens to him. A's almost never happen to Zinkoff, absolutely never in major tests. But this was a major test in Geography, his favorite subject, and somehow he has aced it. In fact, his A is the only A in class—a fact which Mrs. Shankfelder announces while holding up his test paper for all the world to see.

Zinkoff gets an ovation, his first ever. Several kids stand. Barry Haines even whistles, though probably more to show off his whistle than to honor Zinkoff. Congratulations continue to pour in all day. Pats on the back. Playful punches in the arm. Hair mussings. He wonders if it happened because he rubbed his lucky pink bubble-gum stone before taking the test.

In the playground people want to see it. They snatch it from Zinkoff's hand and rub it over their faces and chests and under their arms like a washcloth, rubbing in the A juice, sighing, "Ahhh!" and everyone laughs, and Zinkoff laughs hardest of all.

Like gaudy birds, his name flies in new forms across the schoolyard:

"The Zink!"

"The Z man!"

"The genius!"

"The Zinkster!"

It never occurs to Zinkoff that all the fuss is more than a simple A can account for. It never occurs to him that the loudest and showiest of his congratulators are really not congratulating him at all, but mocking him for blundering into the only A he is ever likely to get.

Zinkoff does not see this.

All he sees is that he seems to have acquired the power to make people happy. The very sight of him brings smiles and twinkly eyes to his schoolmates. Spotting him, boys jerk to a halt, plant their legs as if straddling a motorcycle, thrust a pair of finger-pistols at him and bellow: "There he is!"

Hands sprout like weeds to be high-fived.

"Yo Zink!"

As he comes to the dinner table one night, he stands for a moment at his chair. He thumps his chest with his fist, declares "Ahm da Zink!" and sits down.

His mother and father look at each other.

His sister Polly says, "You da *what*?"

And then this too is over, and like the best friendship, it's over before he knows it. In fact, it has never been quite what he thought it was in the first place.

One day Zinkoff notices that, except for Katie Snelsen and a few others, no one smiles at him anymore. No one is high-fiving him, no one yo-Zinking him. He thinks about it, and he figures he knows why. Field Day is coming. And no one takes Field Day more seriously than fifth-graders. And that's what Zinkoff thinks it is, merely a turning of attention from himself to Field Day. He has heard his last "Yo," seen his last smile. Okay, he thinks, no problem, and he puts on his own game face.

He brings chairs from the kitchen to the back-yard and practices the weave-around-the-chairs race and the one-foot hop and the hiney hop. He goes out onto the sidewalk, and just as he did when he was little, he races cars to the end of the block, and it surprises him that the cars seem so much faster these days. He does jumping jacks.

Meanwhile in school, Gary Hobin is rising to prominence, as he does every year around Field Day time. Field Day is still two weeks away when Hobin goes to Mrs. Shankfelder and asks her to pick the four teams now. "We want to have time to practice together," he says.

So Mrs. Shankfelder writes across the top of the greenboard:

RED YELLOW PURPLE GREEN

Then she writes each student's name on a slip of paper and mixes them in a box. She calls Ronni Jo Thomas up front and tells her to turn her head away and pick a slip from the box. The first name out of the box goes in the RED column, the next name in the YELLOW column, and so on until each student is assigned to a team.

Gary Hobin is a Yellow.

So is Zinkoff.

"Oh no!" blurts Hobin the moment he sees Zinkoff's name go up under his.

The teacher turns from the board. "Pardon me?"

"We can't be on the same team again," says Hobin. "We're supposed to be on different teams each year, to make it fair."

Mrs. Shankfelder frowns. "Don't be silly. There's no such rule."

Hobin snarls under his breath, "There is now."

Ten minutes later Zinkoff receives a note on his desk. The note says, "Forget Yellow. Join another team."

On the playground at lunchtime, Hobin comes to Zinkoff. "Did you get the note?"

"Yeah," says Zinkoff. "What's it mean?"

"It means what it says. You're not a Yellow. Join another team."

"But I *am* a Yellow. Mrs. Shankfelder said so."

Hobin is taller than Zinkoff. He leans down until his eyes are locked into Zinkoff's. Zinkoff can smell the hot dog on his breath. "Listen," says Hobin, "you're not gonna make me lose again. There's no way you're gonna be on my team. Y'understand? Forget it."

Zinkoff is confused. A week ago, Hobin was high-fiving him and calling him "The Zink!" And now this.

"But I practice," says Zinkoff. "I'm good now."

Hobin laughs. "You're a loser. You lose. Go lose with somebody else. You're *not* a Yellow." He walks off, turns back. "And you can't even walk right."

It's in Zinkoff's mind to say "But I got an A!" but he knows it will make no difference.

Each team has a captain, Hobin, of course, being captain of the Yellows. In the days that follow, Zinkoff approaches each of the other team captains and asks if they could use a new member. Each one says no.

Zinkoff does not know what to do.

He is tempted to tell Mrs. Shankfelder of his problem and let her handle it. But he thinks better of it.

He is too embarrassed to tell his parents, to admit that no one wants him on their team.

He rubs his lucky pink bubblegum stone, hoping to change his luck.

And he continues to practice. If anything, he

practices even harder and longer. He is not home for dinner on the last day before Field Day, and his mother has to send Polly out to find him racing cars two blocks away. And even as he gasps for breath walking home, listening to Polly harp at him, he knows what he will do.

He gets up as usual the next day and heads off to school, but he does not arrive. He veers and walks the other way. In the distance he hears the late bell, and he wants to run to it, but he does not. He walks the streets of town. He looks at his feet, trying to see what Hobin sees.

The town is the same and not the same. The same brick housefronts and sidewalks, but no kids. He feels the picture he lives in has been tilted. He has never been so aware of air, the space around him. He feels like he did when he wandered by mistake into the girls' room. (He is the only person he knows to have done so more than once.) A woman across the street in a flowery bathrobe leans from her front door to pick up a newspaper on the step. A yellow cat, emerging from an air-shaft, studies him for a moment and darts back in.

He tries walking the alleys, and that's worse. He's unhappy everywhere. He is nowhere. He wishes to be somewhere. He wishes to be with people. But he cannot go to school, and he cannot go home. Ultimately he walks to the nine hundred block of Willow.

As he heads up the sidewalk he is comforted to see that the Waiting Man is there, even at this strange time of day. He waves to the Waiting Man and aches for a wave in return. It occurs to him to do a silly little dance, to see if the Waiting Man will smile, but he chickens out.

Claudia, the little girl in the harness, is not outside today. He is tempted to knock on the door. "Can Claudia come out and play?" How silly would that sound? Him eleven years old.

"Oh, mailman!"

He turns. She's across the street, leaning on the walker. He runs to her. He wants to hug her, he's so happy she's there.

"Hi," he says.

"Hi," she says. It sounds funny, "Hi" coming from such an old person. He has the impression he could teach her to speak, like a talking bird. She reminds him of a bird, the thin legs sticking out from the bathrobe. School mornings must be the time of bathrobes.

"Come on in," she says. As if she knows he needs to be someplace. She doesn't say, "What are you doing here, it's a school day." She doesn't say, "What's going on?" or "Where's your bike?" She just says, "Come on in," as if this happens all the time.

He goes in.

21 · Something Hard and Thorny

It takes her a long time to climb from the top step into the living room. "You can get the door," she says. He closes the door.

It is dark inside. Not as dark as his cellar, but dark for a house. No lights are on. "So . . ." she says. He waits for the rest, but that's all there is: "So . . ." She repeats it quite a few times as she makes her way across the living room. She sets the four legs of the walker out ahead of her, then catches up with her own two feet. Six legs she has. It's the world's slowest gallop. And then she heads into the dining room. "So . . ." It takes her as long to cross the living and dining rooms as it takes him to walk to school.

"So . . . what would you like?"

What would he like? Not much, really. Take away today and his life has been pretty good.

Then it hits him, they're in the kitchen—she's talking about food.

"Snickerdoodle?" he says. It's the first thing that comes to mind.

She stops. He stops behind her. She cocks her head to one side. "Snickerdoodle? I haven't heard that word in ages. My *mother* used to make snicker-doodles."

He tries to picture the old lady with a mother. He can't. "*My* mother makes snickerdoodles," he tells her.

"No, she doesn't," she says. "They don't make them anymore."

"Well, she *does*," he says.

"No," she says firmly.

"Yes," he says, equally firmly. He's feeling a little annoyed.

She seems to be staring at a leg of the kitchen table. She shakes her head but says nothing. She turns forward in the walker. "Well," she says, "I don't have snickerdoodles." She continues on across the kitchen. "You'll have to ask for some-thing else."

Something else. He can think of many things he would like to eat, but he tries to remember he's not in a restaurant and he's not at home. "A sandwich?" he offers.

"A sandwich." She repeats his words so carefully he wonders if she knows what a sandwich is. He has never been this close to a very, very old person before. He wonders how much there is that such a person does not know. "A sandwich . . . a sandwich . . ." she repeats as she continues her frozen gallop across the kitchen. The back legs of the walker land first with a rubbery thud, then the front legs, then the catch-up shushing of her own slippers on the linoleum. *Thud thud shush shush*. "A sandwich . . ."

He plops into a chair. He is almost woozy from slowness.

She stops at a metal cabinet. "How about peanut butter and jelly?" she says. "Do children still like peanut butter and jelly?"

He has long since outgrown peanut butter and jelly. What he really wants is a pepper and egg sandwich, like his mother makes, with spicy brown mustard. But he guesses this is out of the question. "Sure," he says.

She fusses in the cabinet, fusses in the refrigerator. She finds the peanut butter. "Can't find the jelly," she says. "Today we'll have pretend jelly. How would you like that?"

He's ready to agree to anything. "Okay," he says.

She is so slow, so deliberate in every movement that he sees things he has never seen before. He had not known there were so many steps to the spreading of peanut butter on a slice of bread. Is this how things appear to the Waiting Man, a world in slow motion?

After what seems like hours she heads for the table, pushing the walker with one hand, holding a plated sandwich in the other. When she lays the plate on the table and heads back for the second sandwich, he jumps up. "I'll get it!"

She transfers herself from the walker to a chair, and at long last they set to eating.

"I'm pretending my jelly is gooseberry," she says. She is the color of white mice: pink scalp showing through white hair, pink eyelids. Her eyes are watery, but she is not crying. "We used to have gooseberries on our farm. What's yours?"

"Grape," he says.

"Jelly or jam?" she says.

He is stumped. "Jelly, I guess."

"Jam is easier to spread."

"Okay, jam."

"Are you sure? I always thought jelly had more taste."

"Jelly."

Not that it makes any difference. He really does try to pretend, but all he tastes is peanut butter and bread.

He's glad they're in the kitchen. It's not as dark as the rest of the house. The sandwich halves are in the shape of triangles. He likes it that way. It seems special. Before he knows it his sandwich is gone. The old lady has barely begun. She eats as slowly as she walks.

She looks at him. She puts down her sandwich and with a grimace reaches for the walker. "I'll make you another."

"No," he says. He puts his hand on her wrist.

Her skin feels like newspaper. "I'll do it."

He gets up and makes himself another. "Don't forget the jelly," she calls over her shoulder. He spreads pretend jelly. He slices the sandwich catty-corner, into triangles.

He tries to eat this one more slowly. They do not speak. He wonders about something to drink, but he's afraid to ask.

"Do you know the Waiting Man?" he says.

She tilts her head and sniffs, as if trying to catch the full scent of the question. "Waiting Man?"

"The man at the window, down the street? Nine twenty-four Willow."

She puts down her sandwich, the better to think. She shakes her head. "I don't know any waiting man."

"He's been waiting for a long time," he says. "A *long* time."

He hopes she asks him how long.

She looks at him. Her eyes are gleaming, but he is sure she is not crying. "How long?"

Suddenly he realizes the number is not handy. His father had originally said "thirty-two years."

That was in second grade, he's in fifth now. Three years. Thirty-two plus three . . .

He stares at her. Like stones, he drops each sound into those uncrying eyes. *"Thirty. Five. Years."*

She does not seem impressed. She picks up her sandwich and takes a bite and chews for a long time. Her eyes drift away, toward the living room, the Beyond. "What is he waiting for?" she says.

"His brother."

"Oh." She says this matter-of-factly, nodding, as if that explains everything.

There's a clatter at the front of the house. He realizes it is the mail slot opening, letters being pushed through. His father is delivering. She doesn't seem to hear it.

"What's his name?" she says.

"Who?"

"The brother."

The question surprises him. He has never wondered about the brother's name, or the Waiting Man's for that matter. "I don't know," he says.

She starts in on the second half of her sandwich—he has long since finished his. He feels her staring at him as she chews. He is uneasy. When he looks at her for more than a second at a time, he discovers her skin is almost transparent, like thin ice over a December puddle. He feels he is looking *into* her. A thought pops into his head: The moment she stops chewing she is going to ask him his name.

He does not want her to ask. He does not want her to call out "Oh, Donald!" or "Oh, Zinkoff!" He wants to be "Oh, mailman!"

He must say something, quickly, create a diverting action.

"I can spell tintinnabulation," he blurts. And he spells it for her. He has been waiting for years at school for someone to ask him. "T-I-N-T-I-N-N-A-B-U-L-A-T-I-O-N."

Her mouth drops open, her eyes bulge. She is astonished. She is amazed.

"And I got an A once. In Geography. It was the only A in the whole class."

This time she seems not so much amazed as

pleased. She nods and smiles. She is not surprised. She knew he could do it. "Congratulations," she says.

The echo comes in his parents' words: *One thousand congratulations to you!* And suddenly he remembers the day in the hospital when Polly was born, making a deal with his mother for two stars whenever he really needed them. Could he ever need them more than today?

"Do you have stars?" he says.

She looks at him funny. "Stars?"

"Those little paper stars? Silver? That you stick on—" he is about to say "your shirt"— "paper and stuff?"

She nods. She gets up and goes to a drawer in the cupboard. "Stars . . . stars . . ." she mutters as she roots through the drawer.

She hauls the walker off to the dining room. He regrets he asked.

"Stars . . . stars . . ."

She returns beaming. She's holding up something, but it's not a star. It's a turkey sticker, the size of a postage stamp, the kind Miss Meeks put on a paper of his once or twice. She hands it to him. "How about a turkey?"

A turkey is perfect. He sticks it on his shirt. He can't tell her how happy that turkey makes him feel, so happy now his eyes are watery too, and his breath flutters in his chest and something hard and thorny goes out of him and he tells her everything. He tells her about Field Day and why he isn't at school. He tells her about his two favorite teachers of all time, Miss Meeks and the Learning Train and Mr. Yalowitz who said, "And the Z shall be first!" He tells her about his giraffe hat and Jabip and Jaboop (she laughs out loud at that) and the giant cookie for Andrew Orwell and Hector Binns and his earwax candle. He tells her about Field Day again and what the clocks said and what Gary Hobin said and he tells her about the goal he scored for the Titans and what happened when he closed the door behind him in the cellar with the Furnace Monster which, heaven help him, he still half believes in.

On and on he talks, scooping the fruit out of his life and dropping it into her lap. He gives her his lucky pink bubblegum stone. She rubs it against her dress and gives it back. Through his tears she is blurry, ghostlike. Her white hair sits upon her head like a puff of cotton.

The kid he has always known himself to be seems to be napping nearby. When he wakes up he is on the sidewalk. The lady is calling "Bye, mailman!" from the step and the sun is bright beyond the rowhouse roofs. School is over: Knapsacked kids are racing home. The air feels cool and new, the air feels good upon his face.

22 · Boondocks Forever

The Yellows won big.

Zinkoff finds this out the moment he arrives at school next day. All the Yellows are wearing gold medals around their necks. The medals are really made of plastic, but they look exactly like Olympic gold medals and they hang from their necks on red, white and blue ribbons.

Gary Hobin did great things at Field Day, and for the remaining days of the year he is King of the School. Some days he laughs a lot and is friendly to people whose names he doesn't know. He is never the first one to speak. He has learned that if he holds his tongue, someone will congratulate him. In fact, so many congratulate him that he finds himself surprised when someone does not.

On other days he is serious and is seen stretching and touching his toes during recess and during slow times in class. On these days he does not seem to notice other people. His eyes are focused on the Beyond—certainly not the Beyonds of Binns or the Oh Mailman Lady—most likely the Golden Beyond of Olympic Glory. After a day or two the other Yellows stop wearing their medals to school, but Hobin wears his every day, right up to and including Graduation.

Zinkoff sits with the orchestra during Graduation. The orchestra has two numbers to play, plus "Pomp and Circumstance" as the graduates march in. From his perch on the stage, Zinkoff can see everything, but he cannot locate his parents and sister in the crowd.

The principal says things to get the program started. Then the superintendent of schools speaks. Then comes the orchestra's first number, "Palaggio's Waltz." Twice during the number Zinkoff's flute yips like a pinched sister. The music teacher winces, but Zinkoff never notices.

Then Katie Snelsen receives a book for having the best grades. She stands at the podium and gives a speech. Everyone smiles and pays attention to her. Only the orchestra can see that she is grinding the toe of one shoe into the stage floor.

Next come the awards and special recognitions. There are winners galore—for the best this, the best that, the most this, the most that, second-best, third-best. There are medals and citations and checks and handshakes and gift certificates and trophies and, for Bruce DiMino (Principal's Award), a glass apple.

It is during the giving of the awards that Zinkoff spots Mr. Yalowitz standing in the back. Mr. Yalowitz does not need to be there. He teaches fourth grade, and what does he care about graduating fifth-graders? But there he is, Zinkoff's favorite teacher of all time (along with Miss Meeks) and his end-of-the-alphabet neighbor. And suddenly it hits Zinkoff: He's graduating! No more grade school. No more walking, being first there in the morning; next year he'll ride the bus to middle school. No more staying in the same cozy classroom all day, all year.

For the second time that spring Zinkoff feels

the tears coming. Graduation isn't even over yet, and already he misses John W. Satterfield Elementary. He even misses the boondocks and Field Day and Mrs. Biswell. He looks around. He loves everything and everybody. He wants to hug the walls. The last award is given, and it's time for the orchestra to play "You'll Never Walk Alone." It's just about the hardest thing he's ever done: play the flute and cry at the same time. The music teacher, he notices, seems to be crying too.

He wonders how many of the original two thousand one hundred and sixty days are left. He has never forgotten the number.

Now the principal walks slowly to the podium. He thanks the "talented musicians" for the "wonderful music." He smiles down at the graduates in the front rows. He says, "And now the moment we've all been waiting for."

The graduates stand and head for the stage as the principal calls out the names. The superintendent of schools hands each graduate a rolled-up piece of paper with a blue ribbon around it. The diploma. Most of the graduates grab for the diploma, but the superintendent holds it back and makes them shake his hand before forking it over.

The calling of each name triggers a reaction in the audience. People run crouching down the aisles to snap pictures. Family, relatives, friends cheer the graduate. Some cheers are modest: a little hand-clapping, a "Yea, Sarah!", a "Go get 'em, Nicky!"

Other families are more boisterous: leaping from their seats, arms waving, two-fingered whistles, moose calls, stomping the floor. It's hard not to make comparisons, hard not to notice who gets the loudest cheer, the longest, the most outrageous, the most camera flashes. It's like a last minute, before-you-get-outta-here, final test.

Zinkoff tries not to look at it that way. He knows that some families are simply not as loud as others and that it doesn't mean they love their graduate any less. So it will be with his own family: His father is not a whistler nor his mother a stomper. Still, he can't help thinking it must be nice to have somebody go bonkers over you. That is, assuming you have somebody there to begin with, which he isn't assuming anymore because he *still* hasn't located his parents out there—maybe Clunker Seven broke down—and it's getting to the point where he'll be thankful for just a peep.

Because he's thinking these things and searching the field of faces, he fails to hear his own name called:

"And last but not least, Donald Zinkoff."

The principal waits. The superintendent waits. The principal looks around, as if Zinkoff might be up in the air somewhere. He says it again, this time with a question mark:

"Donald Zinkoff?"

Zinkoff snaps to. He jumps up, lurches for the principal, catches his foot in the chair of the clarinetist beside him and goes sprawling to the floor. The flute goes clattering. The audience explodes with laughter. He doesn't blame them. What a goofus! He joins in the laughter. He scrambles after the flute. He picks himself up, takes a bow and resumes his journey to the principal, only to be reminded that it's the superintendent he needs to see.

By now it is quiet again, and again he is hoping, wondering . . .

The tabletop that had held the stack of diplomas is bare. The last one is in the superintendent's hand. Boondocks forever.

Zinkoff reaches for it but receives instead the superintendent's huge, warm paw. He shakes it. He stands at attention. He declares, "Zinkoff reporting, sir." The superintendent gives him a grin, a brief half salute and, at last, the diploma.

In the audience someone shrieks: "Go Donald!" The voice is familiar. He looks. It's Polly. They've been there the whole time, right in the middle. His parents are clapping with their hands above their heads, but Polly's the one. She's sitting on his father's shoulders and she's flailing her arms and pumping her fists and yelling her face off—"Go Donald! Go Donald!"—and she's doing it, she's going absolutely bonkers, she's giving him the wildest cheer of all. And in the very back of the auditorium, standing against the wall, Mr. Yalowitz smiles and sends him two thumbs-up.

23 · Vanished

Graduation Day is just that: one day.

Then comes the next day.

And the next.

Zinkoff puts away his flute, puts away his backpack, puts away his memories of Graduation Day and gets on with the rest of his life.

To Zinkoff and to all the kids in this brick-and-hoagie town, summer is like a great warm shallow lake. Some frolic and splash. Some strike out for the distant shore, too far away to see. Some just stand there, digging their toes into the sandy bottom. It is warm and sunny and lazy and you can leave your feet if you want to, because in the warm waters of summer, everybody floats.

Zinkoff rides his Clinker One with a new kid from up the block. They cruise the park. They race down Halftank Hill. On his bicycle he is graceful.

For most of July he goes Monopoly crazy. He carries the game with him everywhere, always keeping his favorite piece, the top hat, in his pocket. He gets up games with his parents and with Uncle Stanley and the neighbors and the Oh Mailman Lady. When he can't find anyone else, he resorts to Polly, who begs him endlessly to play. It's never long before his properties cover the board and his stack of money practically scrapes the ceiling. But it's no fun, she's so easy to beat. He tries to make it fun by trouncing her so badly that she'll get mad and stomp off, maybe throw a tantrum, which is always entertaining. But she doesn't. She doesn't seem to care, or even notice, that she's losing. She just loves to roll the dice and loves wherever she lands. He's the one who winds up mad.

Then they go away for summer vacation: three days at the beach. They stroll the boardwalk. He shakes hands with Mr. Peanut and eats an ice-cream and waffle sandwich and a chocolate-covered frozen banana. While Polly digs holes in the sand, he hunkers in the surf and dares the ocean waves to knock him over.

Back home, he pesters his parents to join the swim club, but they say it's too expensive. So he does what a kid has to do: He smells the cedar chest in his parents' bedroom, he decapitates dandelions, seesaws at the park, licks the mixing bowl, rides his bike, counts railroad cars, holds his breath, clucks his tongue, tastes tofu, touches moss, daydreams, looks back, looks ahead, wishes, wonders . . . and before he knows it, miraculously, the summer is over.

Monroe Middle School is scary, it's so big. Four elementary schools feed into it. There are no swings in the playground. There's no playground. No recess. All day long he bounces from room to room, teacher to teacher. Every forty-five minutes it's back into the hallways, the cattle drive. *Moooo!* Eighth-graders tower over him, knock him off balance barging through. When he sees a familiar Satterfield face he beams and waves.

One day the face he sees stops him cold. He calls out, "Andrew!" It's his neighbor from the old days.

Andrew looks but keeps walking. He does not seem to recognize Zinkoff. "It's me. Zinkoff. Donald."

Andrew nods. "Oh yeah. Hi."

Zinkoff runs to catch up. Andrew has really grown since he saw him last. He's five inches taller than Zinkoff. If Zinkoff didn't know better, he'd think he was an eighth-grader. It's not only his height, but the way he carries himself. Unlike most of the other slinky, slumpy sixth-graders, Andrew gives the impression that he belongs here, that he doesn't have to apologize for having been born.

Zinkoff feels a little funny having to look up. "Andrew, you got tall!"

Andrew looks over his head, looks down at him. "Yeah. And it's Drew."

Zinkoff is confused. "Huh?"

"My name's Drew now."

"Oh? You changed it?"

"Yeah."

Zinkoff has never seen Andrew's—Drew's— new home out in Heatherwood, but he can picture it with its driveway and tree out front, and Zinkoff nods, for it somehow seems to add up: new house, new name. "Cool," he says. They're walking side by side now. "Your father still a banker?"

Drew looks down at him. Only his eyes come down, not his face. "Your father still a mailman?"

Zinkoff is about to answer when a bell rings. It's not the one for the next class, it's coming from Drew's backpack. Drew takes out his cell phone and answers it. He's talking away on the phone as he veers off and into his next class.

Zinkoff sits in class—anywhere he wants! He sits front row smack in the middle. He rushes ahead to classes so he can get to the seat first. Every time he sits in the first row, he thinks of Mr. Yalowitz. He misses him.

He joins the band. Meets flutists from the other grade schools. They compare flutes.

He signs up for Camera Club. And Video Club. And Model Car Club. And Library Helpers. But has to drop all except Library Helpers because they interfere with band practice.

He misses a stairway step one day and tumbles

heels to ceiling down to the landing. He's on his hands and knees for minutes picking up pencils, erasers, books, ruler, triangle, multi-template, his lucky pink bubblegum stone, cookie pieces, Monopoly top hat and other spillage from his backpack and pockets. Most students rushing to class zigzag through the disaster. Two eighth-graders, laughing, not noticing, walk straight through, crunching cookies underfoot.

Arithmetic, which had become math, now becomes geometry. Squares and rectangles, okay. But then hexagons, pentagons, octagons, gob-bledeegookgons. He can't get it. He's bad at shapes. He's transferred back to math.

Band is not just band anymore. It's marching band. At first Zinkoff thinks, *Great!* He pictures himself in a fancy uniform, golden braid, doo-dads, a plumed hat high as the old giraffe. But there are no uniforms. You get them in high school. Middle school is for learning the basics.

They practice on the parking lot, learning to play and march at the same time. For the first few days they do a simple straight-ahead march.

Walking and playing. No sweat, thinks Zinkoff.

Then they start on turns. First, a ninety-degree turn. Left, then right. Then forty-five-degree turns. Then about-face turns. Zinkoff cannot seem to get the hang of it. He's okay with either one: He can march without playing, or play without marching. But when he tries to put them together he marches into parked cars, the bike rack, his fellow marchers. It's like bumper cars at the fair. On his worst day he runs into the tuba and bloodies his nose and is told to go home.

But he doesn't give up, and nobody tells him not to come back.

There are two outdoor baskets behind the school. When there's time the kids play pickup games. One of the baskets still has a net hanging from it. The eighth-graders get that one. The other goes to the sixth- and seventh-graders.

Zinkoff hangs around, hoping to get picked. The pickers are always two big-shot athletes. No one elects them. They don't earn it by making foul shots or anything. They simply appoint themselves and no one argues. Gary Hobin is often a picker. So is Drew Orwell.

The pickers stand at the foul line and look over the troops. They take turns picking. You know how good a player a kid is by how early he is picked. When ten players are picked, the unpicked retreat to the sidelines and wait for the game to end—ten baskets—so they can get another chance.

Zinkoff loves basketball now. He keeps waiting game after game. The pickers keep picking, usually the same players. Standing there during picking time, Zinkoff tries to look good. He puts on his game face, he scowls. Anybody can see this kid can score. Once, Drew Orwell looks right at him and he's sure this is it, he can already hear his name, it's forming on Drew's lips— "Zinkoff!"—but the name that comes out is . . .

"Nedney."

And so September becomes October, and October becomes November and December and the grass turns to hairbrushes and the bus riders fog the windows with their breath. The band comes inside and the pickup players come in and the football teams. Halloween. Thanksgiving. Basketball. Tests. Assignments. Projects. Report cards. Cheers. Groans. Waiting for snow.

The school in winter.

And Zinkoff vanishes.

Not to himself, of course. To himself he is very much there, every minute: laughing, burping, biting his pencil eraser. Like everyone else, he is the star of his own life. He is seen and heard almost every day by the other band members and by his sixth-grade friends.

But to the great dragonfly's eye of Monroe Middle School, he is unseen. Even the thing that got him noticed at Satterfield—the losing—is gone. All of that is forgotten, left behind like candy wrappers. The clocks here tell nothing but time. Zinkoff is not a loser here. He is less than that. He is nobody. Long before the first snowfall, he sinks into nobodyness.

24 · Snow

The flake rides in on the fringe of a northwest wind: sails high over Heatherwood before swinging toward the tarpaper roofs of the town, flies over Halftank Hill and Eva's Hoagie Hut and the post office, makes a beeline down Willow Street and on to the grass and asphalt sprawl of Monroe Middle School, dances for a moment outside a second-story window, leaps the spouting and, as if finally tired of it all, falls upon the roof.

In the classroom below, an eighth-grader looks up from the paper where he doodles. He sniffs. He cocks his head. He looks out the window, squints, half rises from his seat. His eyes widen, he throws up his arms:

"SNOW!"

Within seconds the whole school knows.

"It's only flurries."

"That's just the start."

"Could be a blizzard."

"Snow day tomorrow!"

"Pray!"

By lunchtime it's still flurries. The students crowd at the windows of the cafeteria, chanting, "Snow! Snow! Snow!"

"It's only flurries."

"That's all it's gonna do."

"It's tricking us."

"It's not sticking. Look. The ground's dry."

By seventh period a new wind from the south blows the flurries away. The sky is white and still.

"Rats!"

By school day's end wet fat flakes splat on the students' upturned faces as they leap out of school.

"Snow day!"

"Snow day!"

"Snow day!"

Zinkoff loves school, but he loves snow days too, and tomorrow looks sure to be one. As he steps from the bus near his home, he sees that the snow is sticking. The sidewalk is already white. He projects how deep the snow will be on Halftank Hill by tomorrow morning and he shouts, "Yahoo!" forgetting he doesn't say that anymore.

Since it is wet, the snow packs readily into balls, and snowball fights break out up and down the street and all over town. Front steps and car hoods are scraped clean as fast as the flakes can fall.

Three-minute dinners are the rule. Take off your gloves, gobble something down, ignore your mother's grumbling, on with the gloves, back outside, discover: The snow's up an inch!

It's dark by now, and there's something about snow falling under streetlights that makes a kid stop and look. But not for long. Snowballs fly out of the darkness, through the flake-falling tents of light, back into darkness.

The first snowplows come rumbling through. Except it's not a snowplow, it's a tank, and that's a bazooka in your hand. Bam!

Zinkoff is winding up for a tank attack when he first notices the light going by a block away. Then another, flashing red, white and blue. Kids are turning, throwing arms slack. Someone is running.

He joins others heading for the lights. What could it be? Fire? Murder? Snow fights continue, but they're rolling skirmishes now, snow scooped on the run. Over one block, down two, over one.

It's Willow Street. The nine hundred block. It's lit up like a carnival.

Police cars, emergency vehicles: a parade of them up the street, the snowy humps of parked cars pulsing in the swirling lights, people shouting, running, watching from the steps. Hiss of radio voices. The snow is trampled on the sidewalks, rutted in the street.

Zinkoff ricochets like a pinball off milling bodies. Through the glittering snowfall he spots the Waiting Man glowing in his window. He looks like George Washington. He hears fragments:

". . . lost . . ."

". . . little girl . . ."

". . . mother . . ."

". . . freeze . . ."

". . . frantic . . ."

". . . leash . . ."

It's Claudia, the little girl on the leash.

She's lost.

For some reason he's not surprised. He imagines her sneaking off when her mother's back is turned. He imagines her squirming out of the harness, flinging away the leash, throwing her arms in the air with a great "Yahoo!" and bolting into the snow and down the street, free at last, much as he did when he was first allowed outside alone.

The lights cluster brilliantly up the street at Claudia's house. He thinks he sees her mother in the mob at the front step. He hears someone cry out.

He pulls off one glove. He has to do it one finger at a time; it's not easy because the glove is icy and wet. The glove is wet because the balls he has been throwing have been more slushballs than snowballs, because slushballs as everybody knows fly truer and harder, the only problem being they sog up your woolen gloves with icy wetness which, funny, you don't even notice until you stop throwing.

He pulls off the glove and reaches into his pants pocket and takes out his lucky stone, Claudia's gift, the pink petrified clump of bubble-gum. He rolls it in his cold, wet fingers. He remembers a conversation with Claudia's mother. He remembers her saying something funny about being run over by a chicken. He remembers her saying that if Claudia ever started complaining about her leash, they would have to have a chat. He wonders if Claudia complained, or did she just skip that and take off?

He returns the lucky stone to his pocket. The lights are spilling across his eyes.

He begins to pull his glove back on, but the glove is colder than the night air. He removes the other glove. He stuffs them in his coat pockets, then discovers there's no warm place to put his hands. He takes the gloves from his pockets and stands there staring at his hands. He appears to be blushing in the red light spinning atop a nearby truck. He stacks the gloves neatly one upon the other and lays them on the top step of the nearest house.

He starts walking. A snowball hits him in the back.

"Hey, Zinkoff! C'mon!"

The other kids are still battling away. Snow warfare gains a new, thrilling edge when waged in the glare of police lights. Zinkoff walks on.

It seems like the whole town is either on the street or staring from the windows. Everyone is carrying a flashlight. The night is lights and eyes. A toddler in ski pajamas calls from a doorway: "Mommy! Can I look too?" The mother yells, the door slams shut.

The eight hundred block is a little less busy and bright but just as trampled. In the seven hundred block the light comes only from the windows. The search here is quieter: misted breathing, murmurs, the squeak of boots in snow. Once again he is aware of the falling flakes.

Two more blocks, and the sidewalk snow is untouched. He is alone. The words that have been inside him come out now in a whisper: *I will find her. I will find her.*

He walks on.

25 · "Claudia . . ."

The lights from front windows and the lights at the street corners help. It is as if they are looking too. The snowflakes in the light remind him of moths. In the darkness between the lights he cannot see the snow fall. He cannot hear it. He sticks out his tongue to catch a flake.

In the darkness he calls out in a whisper: "Claudia . . . Claudia . . ."

Why he whispers he doesn't know.

Maybe it's because he doesn't want to disturb the night any more than necessary.

Maybe it's so she won't hear him, in case she's having fun.

"Claudia . . ."

The snow is getting deep. It's over his ankles. He wades through it as he waded through the surf at the beach.

It is hard to see between the lights. He whispers into the dark corners.

"Claudia . . ."

The black canyon of housefronts looms over him. Night into night.

"Claudia . . ."

He crisscrosses the street, searching both sides, trying to miss nothing, stitching the sidewalks together.

The falling snow covers everything, makes everything white and soft and humpy. It's a guessing game. What was that? What was that? He thinks she is under the snow. He thinks she is playing a game, waiting to be found. He can almost hear her giggle, searchers so close but not knowing. Or she is asleep. A little girl bear cub asleep under the snow. Every hump he thinks is her. He pokes with his boot, flinches in expectation of her exploding up from the snow, like a flushed bird, laughing. But it's only a sled left outside, a junked TV, a plastic bag of trash.

"Claudia . . ."

Then he thinks, no, she's not still, she's moving,

she's running, rolling in the snow, celebrating. She's unleashed! It's snowing! Unmoving is the last thing she would be.

Every now and then he looks back. The spinning lights are far away now, a fallen spaceship. He loves the distant spinning light. It is his leash. He wishes Claudia had not wanted to be quite so free.

A new light turns the corner ahead. A rumbling. It's a plow, scooping snow like a finger through cake icing. The plow rumbles toward him, its headlights trembling. For the first time in his life he does not reach for a snowball. As the plow passes him an alarming thought occurs: What if she's in the street! He calls out: "Stop!" But the plow rumbles on past and up the street.

Two more blocks and he looks back again. Suddenly he no longer feels he is about to find her any second. All he feels is the silence. He cannot believe how silently the snow falls. He cannot believe she could have come this far. He takes one last look at the distant spinning lights. He turns at the corner. He will go down a block and work his way back toward the light.

Halfway along the block he comes to an alley, and it hits him.

Alley!

The unnamed, unmapped, car-free second streets of the town. Who says she went out the front door into the street, where everyone looks, where every light shines? Who says she didn't bolt out the back door and into the alley? He thinks of the days of his own life spent in the town's alleyways. He feels it, he knows it: This is where she is.

He looks into the blackness. There are no lights here. It is as black as the cellar with the kitchen door shut. This is night's cellar, where night falls to. He takes a step. Another. The light from the nearest streetlamp follows him, loses him.

26 · What a Kid Is

"Claudia . . ."

He sends his whisper out ahead of him. His whisper is his eyes, his fingertips.

"Claudia . . ."

He does not know it is snowing unless he turns his face up.

The snowplow doesn't come here.

He trips over something, sprawls facedown into snow. He gets up, wipes his face. There's snow on his neck, melting under his collar. He takes his hands from his coat pockets, for balance, the better not to fall.

And falls again.

He pulls out his lucky stone. He clutches it in his hand. His hands are wet and cold.

"Claudia . . ."

Dim light ahead: the next street. The snowfall

reappears. He crosses the street and back into alleyway blackness.

"Claudia . . ."

He crosses another street, and another. In time he hears the staticky squawk of a two-way radio. To his right there is light through an air-shaft, glow silhouettes the rooftops. Voices. He is behind Claudia's house. He thinks to call out: "You're looking in the wrong place!" But he only trudges on, leaving the lights and the voices behind, sinking into the blackness.

"Claudia . . ."

He squeezes his lucky stone. He puts his hands in his pockets. His pockets feel the same as his hands, cold and wet. How did that happen?

Squares of light to the left and right show the presence of kitchen and back bedroom windows. But they hold their light, it does not reach the alley. It is flat, like yellow paper pasted on black.

He stumbles in hidden potholes, lurches against open gates and chain-link fences and who knows what all in the cold pillowy night.

He trudges on. He no longer bothers to lift his feet.

"Claudia . . ."

How long can she last? How long can a little girl stay warm, stay alive in a snowstorm at night?

He will find her.

How will he find her?

Will she be crouched and shivering, something he stumbles over?

Will he hear her first, hear her little girl voice laughing and saying, "I runned away! I runned away!"

What will he say when he finds her? He thinks. He thinks. He will say "Aha!" That's all he can think of.

Will she want to have a snowball fight before they go home? Will he say, "Don't be silly"? Will she insist?

He thinks of Polly, his sister. Polly was once as little as Claudia. Polly used to run away too. "Gets it from Donald," his mother used to say. But that wasn't true. Donald didn't run away. He left the house. There's a difference. Polly *ran away*.

When Polly got a notion, it was "Katie, bar the door," as his mother used to say. Maybe she should have said, "Katie, get the leash." But there was no leash and no harness, and if the door wasn't barred, it was Polly down the steps and up the street.

Whoever was closest, that was your job: Get Polly. His father used to say, "Some day I'm going to call her bluff. I'm going to let her walk as far as she wants." Uncle Stanley said, "I bet she'll walk all the way to Cleveland."

And one day darn if his father didn't do it, called her bluff, let her go. He stayed right behind her, Donald behind him. When she came to the street she just waltzed on across it, no stop, look and listen for her, his father like a mother duck, watching for cars. When she realized he was behind her, she squealed and ran faster, her little rear end bouncing like a pair of apples.

She didn't make it all the way to Cleveland, but she did make it to Ludlow Avenue, which his father bragged for the next several years was at least a mile from where she started. But in the end she stopped. Funny thing, she never slowed down, she just stopped, in the middle of the street. She stopped and turned and looked at him and his father and just plopped her apples right down on the street, one car coming to a stop, another swinging around them.

She had been utterly pleased with herself. "I runned away!" she chirped, and the sun was no match for her smile. And Zinkoff saw in that moment something that he had no words for. He saw that a kid runs to be found and jumps to be caught. That's what being a kid is: found, caught. Then she did something that has never left him. Sitting there in the middle of the street, she reached up to him, not to his father but to him, and his heart went out of him and he picked her up and he carried her home on his shoulders.

"Claudia . . ."

She isn't running anymore. He knows that now. She is waiting.

The lucky stone—he cannot feel it. Did he drop it? He panics. When he comes to the next street light, he looks. The stone is still there, in his hand. His hands have become like the stone, cold and hard and unfeeling. He lifts the stone and runs its smooth, icy surface along his cheek. He runs it along his lips. He puts it in his mouth, the only warm part of him left.

Back into the blackness.

"Claudia . . ."

27 · Himself

He comes to the end of the alley. He goes down the street, up another alley, sucking on the bubblegum stone, keeping it warm. He blows on his fingers.

He looks up. He can no longer feel the flakes on his face, except on his lips. He wishes he could see the stars. He still thinks of them as his stars. He remembers one of his earliest beliefs, that a number of stars fell to earth each day so that mothers could go about gathering them for their children's shirts. He wishes he still believed it. He stops, faces full to the sky. He closes his eyes, feels the flakes on his eyelids: cold ash of dying stars.

He wants to stop. He wants to go to sleep. He thinks of his bed. He pictures himself in his pajamas. No, first he pictures himself in the bath-tub. He has been taking showers because he's big now, but for this one more time he wants the bath. He lets the water run and run, and his mother doesn't call up, "Donald, that's enough! Turn it off!" not this time. He lets the warm water rise all the way to his belly button before he turns it off, then he slinks down into the steamy ever-lasting warmness, only his head above. And then into bed, under the covers, curled up, shivering not from cold but with delight, giggling under his soft warm mountain of covers . . .

He stumbles over something, goes lurching into a chain-link fence. The fence rattles, then spills its dislodged snow with a sound like breath going out.

He yells, he screams down the trench of blackness:

"Claudiaaaaaa!"

Silence.

Surprisingly, the top of his head is not cold. His hair is thick, and the snow that falls upon it keeps getting shaken off by his repeated stumbles and fallings. But his ears, they are freezing. The crests of his ears are so cold they feel as if they're burning. He muffs them with his hands, but his hands are as cold as his ears. He's going to get hollered at good when he gets home. His mother is always telling him not to go out in weather like this without his hat. She's going to say "Heaven help me" at least fifty times.

He thinks of the Waiting Man. He wonders if the Waiting Man ever thought of going over to Vietnam and looking for his brother himself. And then it occurs to him: Maybe he did. Maybe he did go over there, as soon as he heard his brother was missing in action. Maybe he figured he was the best one to go looking for his own brother, and maybe he went tramping up and down the jungle till his shoes wore out, and maybe he was on his second or third pair of shoes when they kicked him out because it was their jungle not his, and so that's why he came back to the window, he had no choice.

And he sees the front window of Claudia's house, across the street from the Waiting Man, and he sees Claudia's mother, hears a voice from the future, "Yeah, it's a shame. One night during a snowstorm the little girl ran off. Used to wear a harness. Just took off. Whole town came out looking for her, even the Zinkoff kid. They looked and looked. Turned this town upside down. Never could find her. Now look, her mother sits in that window, waiting for her little girl to come home. Been waiting there for over thirty years . . ."

He bites down hard on his lucky stone.

"Claudia . . ."

He comes to the end of this second alley and finds a third and comes to the end of that and finds another. Before one turn he sees red-and-white spinning lights in the distance. He no longer wants to scold them for looking in the wrong place. Seeing the lights makes him feel good now, makes him feel part of a team as he heads down the next alleyway.

He hasn't noticed, but the back house lights have gone out along the way, the kitchens and bedrooms. He does notice, however, that something is different. Noise. The snow has become noisy. A vast brushy noise all about him as of a broom sweeping. He lifts his face, he feels tiny prickles on his skin. It's not snow, but it's not rain either. Within minutes the soft sweeping sound has become a chittering, as if someone above is sprinkling salt on the world. His footsteps crunch. He reaches down. The top of the snow has become crusty, slick and cold and crusty. Not good for making snow angels. He should have made a snow angel before the snow got crusty. He wonders if Claudia is making snow angels. He wonders if angels are invisible in the snow. He wonders if angels make people in the snow. He wonders if Claudia is an angel . . .

The tiny grains of ice have turned to freezing rain that pelts his face and runs down his neck and onto his shoulders and wakes him up, which is quite a surprise since he didn't know he had gone to sleep in the first place. But here he is, lying not standing in the snow. He tries to push himself up, but his hand breaks through the crust, and snow like cold cotton runs up inside his coat arm past his elbow. He jumps up. He flaps his arm violently to shake out the snow. The snow falls out, but try to get his icicle of an arm to believe it.

He trundles onward. His head is soaking wet.

He's taking a shower. "Hey Mom, I'm taking a shower!" Does he say it or think it? He's not sure. He's not sure of a lot of things anymore. Things seem to be blending, differences disappearing. He is no longer sure where he ends and the snow begins. Snow is him. Cold is him. Night is him.

He knows himself only by the stone in his mouth, the last faintly glowing ember of what used to be Zinkoff. He clamps the stone in his teeth, covers it with his tongue. He stomps once through the crust, trying to shake the rest of himself loose from the night.

He stomps again and barks into the night: "Claudia!"

Now she's made him mad. "Wait till I get a hold of you."

A gleam of light. A distant voice. A funny siren, sounds like a hiccup. He calls: "I'm looking here! You look there! We'll find her!"

Or does he just think he calls?

He reminds himself, reminds himself.

Claudia's mother.

The Waiting Man.

One Waiter is enough. There will be no more

Waiters on the nine hundred block of Willow. "Period!" he says out loud.

And falls asleep. He's still walking, but he's asleep as surely as any of those people behind the back house windows. And why not? It's so easy when you are the night and the night is you and you're down to the last stone in your mouth and there's nothing to see anyway—it's all black!—so where's the difference between an eye open and an eye closed?

Until you walk into a garage door.

He bounces rudely off the door and falls on his back into the snow. He's up and slogging onward, turned around now in the confusion and heading back the way he came.

"Claudia . . ."

Walking . . . walking . . .

Thud thud shush shush

"Oh, Mailman!"

He looks up. She smiles. "Come on in," she says, and he goes in. And what a wonderful surprise: It's hot chocolate time! There's his old Winnie the Pooh mug from when he was little. She pours in the hot chocolate all foamy and steaming, and then comes the best part, the Cool Whip. She scoops some on but not enough, never enough, because it's his mother now and she's playing the game, she's waiting for him to say "More!" so he says it and she piles on more, and he has to practically sink his whole face into the Cool Whip to get down to the hot chocolate, and it's heaven it's a car . . .

He has sleepwalked onto a street and into a parked car.

He trundles on. He thinks he's in an alley but he's in the middle of a street. He hears a squawk. The hiccuping siren. He sees a flashing light— red, blue. He's glad they're still out looking for her. He thinks they will find her first.

The rain is coming down harder now, he can hear it, the sound is so much louder. He squints. He tries to see the rain in the streetlight, but he cannot seem to focus. He holds out his hand. He tries to look at it, but his hand will not stay still. He looks up. Nothing falls on his face. The rain has stopped. The snow has stopped. If not the rain, what is that noise?

It's himself. His teeth. They're chattering,

rattling worse than Clunker Nine, shaking like his hand, like his whole body, the lucky stone dancing in his mouth.

Zinkoff is cold.

Pretending is warm.

He pretends he's his dad. With every step he says, "Piece a cake . . . piece a cake . . ." He lurches into another car. He punches himself to stay awake. He stomps. He can't feel his toes. Who took his toes? He sings: "Somebody took my toes . . ." He sings: "Claudiaaaah . . . oh Claudiaaaah . . ." He must stay awake, must stay awake, must find her, no more waiting. He spells his favorite word, he calls it out loud to the chitterchattering night: "T-I-N-T-I-N-N-A-B-U-L-A-T-I-O-N." He sings it: "T-I-N-T-I-N-N-A-B-U-L-A-T-I-O-N." He hears Claudia calling. She's on Halftank Hill, she's on his sled, on his back, and they're sailing down the hill and she's screaming, screaming, she's Polly, sitting on his dad's shoulders screaming "Go Donald! Go Donald!" And he goes, he blazes like the wind down the sidewalk racing the cars, beating them to the end of the block. "And the Z shall be first!"

declares Mr. Yalowitz. "And the Z shall be last!" declares Mrs. Biswell and the Waiting Man winks in the window and says, "Pass me a snicker-doodle." Yellow button, yellow button, what do you say? "Get off my team," says the yellow button. One thousand congratulations. Gimme a T! Gimme an I! Gimme an N! . . . Whaddayagot? Candles! Get yer candles here! Genu-wine ear-wax candles, two thousand one hundred and sixty congratulations apiece! Two thousand one hundred and sixty . . . two thousand one hundred . . . All aboard! Allll aboard! Next stop Jabip Jabip Jabip good morning young citizens good morning good morning heaven help heaven help help . . .

The lights are blinding him. The lights are rumbling. He knows that he must turn away, he must get to the alley, he must find Claudia, but he cannot get away from the lights, he cannot move, and a whistle is screaming and a voice is saying, "Hold on, son, I gotcha . . ."

28 · Grounded

Voices.

And a sound like scissors: *ssnp ssnp.*

He is warm. He doesn't want to look. It is warm and safe behind closed eyes.

". . . never saw anything like it. Good thing I was paying attention." A man's voice he thinks he's heard before. In the distance but he hears it clearly.

"He didn't say why?" His father's voice.

"Didn't say anything. Prob'ly couldn't anyway, way he was shaking. Funny though, when I stopped and got out, I swore I heard him singing."

"And you knew who it was?" His mother.

"Well, I figured. I mean, who else could it be? He fit the description. Heightwise, anyway. Otherwise he looked like a drowned rat."

"And you were on the lookout." His mother. "You heard the description, and you were going slow and you were keeping an eye out."

"No more'n everybody else."

"One good thing after another." His father.

"I was you, I couldn't wait to ask him why."

"He's been doing that all his life." Uncle Stanley. "Running from the house. Can't keep him tied down. Always going. Used to believe he didn't sleep. Used to sneak out of the house to get to school early. Early!"

"Not me."

Chuckles.

"Me neither. But that's him. His sister too. When she was two she walked halfway to Cleveland one day."

"To Ludlow Avenue."

"Far enough."

Laughter.

And he thinks: "Claudia!"

His eyes are open. He's in his parents' bed. Polly is kneeling beside him with a pair of scissors. She gawks at him. She bolts from the bed and yells downstairs. "Mommy, Mommy, he's awake!"

Good-byes are said, the front door opens and closes, footsteps coming.

They're all in the room: his parents, Polly, Uncle Stanley. His mother sits on the bed. She feels his forehead. "I can't believe you don't have a fever."

He is speaking, but his mother overlays his voice with hers: "Donald, what were you *doing* out there?"

The question is almost too silly to answer, but he answers anyway. "Looking for Claudia." He adds, to show them how silly, "Like everybody else."

They're staring at him, funnylike, all four of them. Uh-oh, he thinks, they *still* didn't find her.

Now they're looking at each other.

"Claudia?" his mother says.

"The little lost girl last night," explains Uncle Stanley. "That's her name."

The look on his mother's face is scaring him. Her eyes are sparkling directly above his. Her voice is almost down to a whisper. "You were looking for the little girl?"

He nods, afraid to speak, afraid something will break.

"At one o'clock in the morning? All that time?"

He nods again. Her face is really scaring him now. So is his father's. Uncle Stanley turns away. He says, "He doesn't know."

She's dead.

"Donald—" His mother's hands are cupping his face. He feels her breath. "The little girl was found shortly after she got lost."

"Found her in somebody's car, in the garage," says his father. His voice is hoarse. "Door wide open. She was pretending to drive."

Uncle Stanley clears his throat. "She was back in her house by, what, seven thirty? Eight o'clock, tops?"

His father nods. "Yep."

His mother is doing a trick with her face: It is sad and smiley at the same time. "But you didn't know that, did you? You just kept looking and looking."

He nods.

Then starts remembering, and the more he remembers the more confused he becomes. "But I saw lights. And sirens." She's looking down on him, crying and smiling. So if Claudia was found, back home safe and sound by eight o'clock, tops . . .

He looks up into his mother's sad and happy smile. He says, "Who were they looking for?"

And reads the answer at once in her face, but waits anyway for her to say it:

"You, Donald. They were looking for *you*."

For the longest time the room is nothing but eyes. His mother, his father, his sister, Uncle Stanley—all staring at him, as if he will disappear if they don't. He's in a cradle of eyes.

Polly pokes him. "Yeah, dummy, *you*."

And then the bed rocks and rolls as they all jump aboard. They're squeezing him and mussing his hair, and Polly is shrieking, "You're sitting on it!" She pulls something out from under his father, the thing she has been cutting with the scissors, a large piece of white paper cut to a fancy design. She unfolds it, holds it up proudly for him to see.

Uncle Stanley gives a groaning chuckle. "Just what he needs. Another snowflake."

For the first time since he opened his eyes, he notices the light streaming through the bedroom windows. And remembers: "Are we having a snow day?"

"Ever since it came over the radio," says his father, "six thirty this morning."

He cheers weakly—"Yahoo!"—then looks at the windows again and thinks to ask, "What time is it?"

"Almost three in the afternoon," says his mother. "You've been sleeping for thirteen hours."

Oh no! Only two hours of daylight left. Halftank Hill!

He tries to leap from the bed but is caught in a web of arms.

"Not today, pal," says his father. "You are grounded."

"Yeah, pal," says Polly, shaking her finger in his face, looking stern.

"For the rest of today."

"Yeah!"

"And you're going to *stay* grounded if I have to sit on you."

"Yeah!"

Polly applauds. And now there's an evil grin on her face and she's reaching into her pocket and pulling out . . .

"My lucky stone!" He snatches at it, she pulls it away, sticks out her tongue. He whines, "Mom!"

His mother holds out her hand. "Give." Polly gives.

"Mom, drop it!" He yells this so suddenly she does just that, she drops it onto the bed. "You can't touch it." He picks it up.

She looks hurt. "But I'm your mother."

She doesn't understand. A lucky stone loses its power if other people touch it. "Nobody can touch it but me."

He stashes it under the pillow.

"Is that thing what I think it is?" his mother says.

"Bubblegum."

"I thought so."

"See?" Polly sneers. "It's not even a stone." She juts her face at him. "And it ain't lucky. And it was in your mouth! *Eewwwwww!*"

"Do you want to tell us why it was in your mouth?" his mother says.

He thinks for a moment. "No, I guess not."

His mother smiles. "Okay."

Polly whines, "Mom, make him tell!"

"I'm making you get off this bed." She pulls Polly off. "Give your brother some peace. You were sure nice to him as long as he was sleeping. Now shoo."

Polly stomps from the bedroom.

The phone rings. It's Aunt Sibyl. She wants to know how the patient is doing.

Then it's Aunt Janet calling. Then Cousin Marty and Cousin Will and Aunt Melissa. When the doorbell starts ringing—first in is Mrs. Lopresti, the new neighbor—he's allowed downstairs to be bundled up on the sofa. For the rest of the day and evening neighbors and relatives come and go. There's talk and laughter and food all over the place.

Almost every person has the same question: "Why?" What was he doing out there? they want to know. And when his parents tell them why, they turn to him and stare at him funny; then they come over and some sit on the edge of the sofa and some just bend down, and they're all smiling that half-sad sort of smile his mother had upstairs, and they all seem to have to reach out and touch him. He can't remember ever being touched so much.

Somewhere in there among all the ringing doorbells and laughter, he looks up and it's Claudia and her mother standing there. Claudia pounces on him and kisses him loudly a dozen times. Then she says something to him. He can't understand her words, but he doesn't have to, he feels them. As for Claudia's mother, she doesn't say "Why?" like the others. She says nothing. She just sits on the sofa and pulls him into herself and won't let him go.

All in all, there's so much going on that he pretty much forgets he slept through a snow day.

29 · Still There

It's almost ten o'clock when the last of the visitors leave and the party's over. His parents come and sit on the rug by the sofa and tell him how it happened the night before.

"You didn't come home when you were supposed to," says his mother.

"As usual," his father cuts in.

"But we weren't worried at first. We thought you were out playing in the snow. But then it was eight thirty, nine o' clock, and you still weren't home."

"That's when we officially started to worry."

His mother called the homes of kids he might be playing with while his father started trekking the streets, calling his name. They really didn't want to call the police. Only an hour before, there had been all that commotion over the little lost girl on Willow Street, and now they knew how it would sound: Guess what? Another one's lost.

But when it's dark and the streets are deserted and every kid in town is safe and snug at home except yours, you don't care how it sounds, you call the police. And they came, like a flashing army, the same police cars and rescue trucks and emergency vans that had been out for the little girl only hours before. Now it was their street lit up like a block party.

"Only it wasn't like the little girl," says his father. "We weren't finding you fast. And the snow was coming down, turning into sleet, then rain."

"You were out looking too, right, Dad?" he says.

His dad looks at him. "Yeah, I was out."

"Piece a cake for you, right?"

He's thinking of his father delivering the mail in all kinds of weather. He's remembering how he used to sit in school and picture his dad hunched like a fullback punching a hole in whistling blizzards.

His father gives him a lopsided smile and a squeeze on the knee. "Yeah, piece a cake."

They tell him how slowly the minutes and hours passed, and how long Polly tried to stay awake but finally couldn't. There are things they tell him and things they do not tell him, and when they come to the end, when the man in the snow-plow finds him far from home and brings him back, and the rescue squad takes over the house and gets him dried and warm and checked out "stem to stern" and he's just floppy dopey like a zombie and they're both so happy and his mother is "bawling like a baby," when they come to the end of the end, how they carried him upstairs and put him right into their own bed between them— by then there's a smile on his face and he's feeling something he hasn't felt in years, like he's little again, like he's been hearing a bedtime story.

"So," says his father, "just where were you, anyway, all that time? Where were you looking?"

He shrugs. "Alleys, mostly." There seems no need to say more.

They stay up until midnight. "I know you're not tired," his mother says, "but why don't you just give it a try anyway. See what happens."

He asks them if he can stay downstairs and sleep here on the sofa. He's getting to like it.

They look at each other and finally say okay, as long as he promises not to go sneaking out the door as soon as they turn their backs.

They kiss him good night, one final hand on his forehead, and upstairs they go.

The house is dark and quiet, everything is dark and quiet but the inside of his head. In there it's still party time; the phone is ringing, the pizza dripping. In there it's still snowing and still raining, and still he treks the alleyways looking for Claudia. But now it's almost fun, because the rest of him is plenty warm and on the sofa, and Claudia got found by eight o'clock, tops.

He closes his eyes and gives it a try. Not much happens, but he keeps trying. He hums a lullaby to himself. In the dark a few small muscles here and there continue to stir: They do not want to sleep, they want to be out in the alleys, searching.

And it comes to him, what he needs to do. He gets up. He wears the blanket like a robe. In the dark he feels his way to the front door. He feels for the deadbolt latch. He turns it slowly, as silently as he can, holding his breath. He turns the knob, silently, slowly. He opens the door. He leans out, trying to keep his feet on the carpet inside. The night air is cold on his neck. He leans out as far as he can and looks up. He smiles. The sky is clear. They're still there. The stars.

He comes back in, closes the door. Once again on the sofa, he pulls the covers snugly about him and in minutes is fast asleep.

30 · "Zinkoff"

After the snow day comes the weekend, and by Monday much of the snow is gone. It remains only in the shadows and corners and north-facing surfaces of the town, and on the edges of large parking lots, where the plows have shoved the snow into small gray mountains. The temperature is up to the low fifties, warm for December, and in gutters and alleys all over town water trickles toward sewers and drains.

Best of all, Monday is in-service day at Monroe Middle School. There's something special about playing just outside the school doors while all the teachers have to be inside. Kids are swarming: hockey on the parking lot, football and soccer on the fields, goofing off all over in the balmy weather.

Under a canopy of arcing footballs, two kids,

Tuttle and Bonce, are having a discussion. Tuttle is pointing. "See him? That kid there?"

He's pointing to a kid in a yellow baseball hat. "Yeah."

"Watch this."

Tuttle calls for a ball. He spins the ball in his hand, he fingers the laces. "Watch." He calls out to the kid. "Hey—yo—here ya go!" He winds up and fires a trim spiral at the kid. The kid reaches out with both hands as if he's about to take a baby from someone's arms. The ball passes neatly through the kid's hands and drills him in the chest. The kid's hat flies off. He staggers backward, almost falling. He scrambles to retrieve the ball and hat.

Tuttle and Bonce share the chuckle of the superior athlete among the underblessed.

"What a spaz," says Bonce. "Look at him. He throws like a girl."

"He throws like a *baby* girl."

"Who is he?" says Bonce.

"Who knows?" says Tuttle.

They watch as the kid calls, reaches out for

someone to pass another ball to him. Finally someone does. This time the ball bounces off his head. Again his hat goes flying.

Tuttle and Bonce crack up, howling.

Tuttle calls, "Yo, Hobin! C'mere!"

Hobin joins them.

"Watch this," says Tuttle. Tuttle calls for a ball and does what he did before, he whips a hard one at the kid in the yellow hat. Again the kid reaches out, and again the ball passes through his hands and nails him in the chest.

Hobin doesn't seem amused. He sneers. "Coulda told ya."

The three of them watch as the kid this time tries to punt the ball back to them. On his first try, his foot misses the ball altogether. On his second try, the ball travels some ten feet in the air.

"So who is he?" says Bonce.

"His name's Zinkoff," says Hobin. "He went to my school. He's nobody."

"Yeah, but didn't you hear about him?" It's Janski, who has joined the group.

"Hear what?" says Bonce.

"About that little girl that got lost the other night?"

"Yeah?"

"This kid goes out looking for her, right? So they find her, like just a little while after she got lost?" The others nod. "So the little girl is home and all, and everybody else goes home, the search is over, okay? But *this* kid"—he nods toward the kid in the yellow hat—

"Zinkoff," says Bonce.

"Yeah, he don't know it. The search is over and he don't know it."

The four of them turn to look at the kid.

Bonce says, "The little girl is home all safe and found and he's still out *looking* for her?"

Janski grins into Bonce's face. He says it slowly:

"For . . . seven . . . hours."

Tuttle shrieks. "Seven *hours*?"

"Seven . . . hours," Janski repeats. "A snowplow found him at two o'clock in the morning. Almost ran him over. He was two miles from home."

Bonce stares at the yellow-hatted kid, who again is trying to punt a ball. "He musta been half dead."

"He musta been half stupid," says Tuttle. "How stupid is that, looking till two o'clock in the morning for somebody that's already found."

Hobin sneers. "Coulda told ya."

"Was he froze?" says Bonce.

Janski shrugs.

"What a wipeout," says Tuttle.

"Shoulda seen him Field Day in fourth grade," says Hobin.

"Yeah?" says Tuttle. "Bad, huh?"

Hobin does not answer. They all stare at the kid, who is now running this way and that, trying to entice someone to throw him a ball. They try to picture how bad it was.

"And he *likes* school. He goes early."

Everyone turns to stare at Hobin, who has spoken these words. They keep staring at him, waiting for him to say he was kidding. But Hobin says nothing else. They turn their attention back to the kid in the yellow hat, who seems not to know he's being stared at.

At last Bonce says, "So, let's get a game."

Everybody breaks from the trance. "Yeah!"

Tuttle calls, "Game! Game!"

Kids who want to play come running.

Teams are chosen. Tuttle and Bonce are the captains. They flip fingers for first pick. Tuttle wins.

"Hobin," he says.

"Janski," says Bonce.

They go on choosing sides—Tuttles here, Bonces here—until the only one left is the kid in the yellow hat. But the sides are even. Tuttle and Bonce have each chosen seven kids. Yellow Hat is a leftover.

But this kid's not acting like a leftover. A normal leftover would see that he's one too many, that everybody but him has been picked and that therefore he must be pretty hopeless and therefore he better just get on out of there and go play something he's good at, like Monopoly.

But this kid just stands there. He shows no sign of turning and vanishing. And he's not *just* standing there, he's *staring* at Tuttle and Bonce.

Tuttle says, "*We* got enough."

So now the kid is just staring at Bonce. And Bonce wants to say "*We* got enough," but he can't seem to say it. He wishes the kid would just turn and go away. Doesn't he know he's a leftover?

Hobin's voice rings out from the other side: "Tackle!"

They usually play two-hand tag. There are no pads, no helmets. And half the field is muddy from the melted snow. But no one objects. No one wants to appear to be afraid to play tackle.

Janski speaks: "The sides are even up. We don't need nobody else."

The kid does not take the hint.

This is uncharted territory: a leftover who won't go away. Still, Bonce holds the power. All he has to do is open his mouth. *Please, go,* he thinks. The kid is still staring at Bonce. The kid really *is* stupid. The kid doesn't know that even if he's allowed in he's only going to be ignored. Or embarrassed. Or hurt. He doesn't know that he's a klutz. Doesn't know he's out of his league.

Doesn't know a leftover doesn't stare down a chooser. Doesn't know he's supposed to look down at his shoes or up at the sky and wish he could disappear, because that's what he is, a leftover, the last kid left.

But this kid won't back off, and his stare is hitting Bonce like a football in the forehead. In those eyes Bonce sees something he doesn't understand, and something else he dimly remembers. It occurs to him that he wants to ask the kid what it was like, those seven hours. He thinks he must be able to see them in the kid's eyes, some sign of them, but he cannot. He wants to ask the kid what it was like, being that cold.

This is goofy, he thinks. He thinks of a thousand things to say, a thousand other ways this could go, but in the end there's really only one word, he knows that, one word from him and who knows where we go from there?

He points, he says it: "Zinkoff."

And the game begins.